"I love to read accounts of history from views of people who care. This was enjoyable. Light and easy reading."

"The story of the birth of our Lord is known far and wide. This well-written [book] tells the story from Mary and Joseph's view. I loved it!"

"To be able to read a story of Mary as she, just a child, is told by an angel of God that she would be the mother of the Messiah! And then to follow the next nine months with her, through her doubts and fears is astounding. Joseph, her husband to be, has his serious doubts [and] to follow their struggles and their love for each other was such a joy. Wonderful read!"

Other Books By The Author

After The Call

Speak Tenderly To Her

Stay With Me

Stepmother's Anonymous

The Book of Joy

Ruth E. Griffin

FULL OF GRACE

Studio Griffin
A Publishing Company
www.studiogriffin.net

For my family

Table of Contents

Glossary of Terms

Abba: Affectionate term for Father

Achichem: Brother

Achot: Sister

Av: July/August

Bat-doda: Female cousin

Binah: God's idea of spiritual perfection

Dod: Uncle

Doda: Aunt

Erusin: Betrothal period

Goy/Goyem: Non-Jew, Gentile

Heshvan: October/November

Imma: Affectionate term for Mother

Ishah: Wife

Iyar: April/May

Iyshah: Husband

Ketubah: A legal, binding document detailing the husband's obligations to his wife

Kiddush: Wine

Kislev: November/December

Mashiac: Messiah

Malakh: Angel

Nechadni: Niece

Nekhed: Grandchild

Nisan: March/April

Nissuin: Marriage ceremony

Rabbi: Teacher

Savta: Grandmother

Sheva Berakhot: The seven blessings

Sivan: May/June

Tammuz: June/July

Tevet: December/January

Jewish Calendar

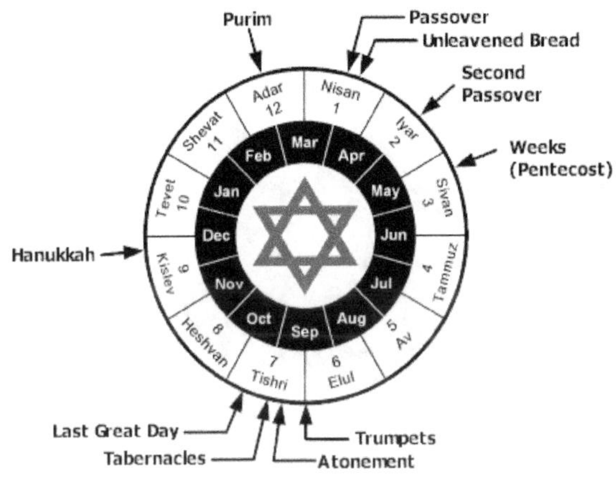

Source: http://catholic-resources.org/Bible/Festivals.htm

Author's Note

The custom of substituting the word "God" with "G-d" in English is based on the traditional practice in Jewish law of giving God's Hebrew Name a high degree of respect and reverence. When written or printed, God's Hebrew Name (and many of the stand-in Names used to refer to God) cannot be erased or destroyed. And while there was no prohibition against pro-nouncing God's Name in ancient times, the name "*Adonai*" or "Ha-Shem" (literally The Name) was often used instead.

1 *Nisan*

"MARY AND JOSEPH, HUGGING AND kissing…"

Mary blushed at her sisters' teasing and tried to quiet them, but they only made faces at her. She had grown accustomed to this kind of behavior from them, as her sisters were much younger and more immature than she. However, she did not appreciate their conduct now that Joseph was waiting to see her. Mary decided it was probably best to ignore them, and joined her father and Joseph outside. She kept her eyes on the ground below, and waited for either of them to speak.

"Hello, Mary," Joseph said

Mary looked up at her betrothed. He was tall and lean, with black hair and a close beard, unlike the full, bushy one her father had.

"Hello, Joseph," she managed to reply, her eyes locked on his.

"Joseph was just telling me how well his shop is doing," her father, Heli, interjected.

"My *abba* did the hard work in establishing it. I'm only following his legacy," Joseph replied.

"You shouldn't be so modest," Heli stated, patting the young man on his shoulder. "You've done well for yourself and for your *imma*."

Joseph nodded his head and the moment seemed to pass. An awkward silence surrounded them, and Mary looked down at the ground again, wishing she could be alone with Joseph. Such a thing was not possible though. Mary had her reputation to protect: she was a virgin and would remain so until her *nissuin*. Still, there were days she desired the end of their *erusin*, so she could go home with Joseph as his wife.

Mary cleared her throat, unintentionally breaking the silence. Heli motioned to Joseph, who presented Mary with a small package.

"Oh, I brought this for you," he said.

Mary took the cloth-wrapped gift and gently unpacked it. Inside was a small, wooden bird, life-like in nature and appearance. She ran her fingers over the intricately carved piece, marveling at the skill it took to make it and the care in Joseph's heart for her.

"Thank you," she said, making eye contact with him again. It was tradition for the groom to bring his intended gifts during the *erusin*, so she wouldn't forget him, but as Mary peered into his eyes, she knew this was not something she would do: she looked forward to marrying Joseph and living her life as his wife.

3 *Nisan*

"THANK YOU, *ADONAI,* FOR MAKING ME according to your will."

Mary listened as her mother, Anna, began the morning prayer. She knew the words by heart because they had been taught to her when she was younger. These words offered her comfort in a G-d who made her a woman and gave her great *binah.* He had also given her a loving family and a hope for a future with a caring man. Despite their struggles as a people with the Roman *goyem,* she was grateful for her life and everything in it.

"Mary," Anna said, calling her attention back to the present. "Finish."

Mary straightened up and uttered the words she had prayed for years: "I am available to you, *Adonai,* that I might be the mother of your *Mashiac.*"

"So be it," Anna concluded.

"So be it," Mary, Oprah and Kyla repeated.

They rose and began their day. There were chores to be done and the morning meal to prepare before her father, Heli, and brother, Nathan, returned from the morning blessing at the synagogue.

"Run to the well and get more water," Anna asked of her, as she brought out the flour.

Mary obliged and grabbed her shawl. She covered her hair and picked up the large, ceramic pot beside the door. Though the day had barely begun, the sun was already out in full force. Mary blinked and started towards the well. It was a fifteen-minute walk there, past the homes and neighbors she had known her whole life. She strolled past a goat farm and into the field, where the well was located. It was dug in her grandparent's day and still flowed with water. She stopped at the stony exterior of the well and set her pot down. Her thoughts on the task-at-hand, Mary proceeded to fill it up with water, knowing it would not be enough to last the entire day. She would have to return.

"Hail, Mary, full of grace. You are blessed among all women."

Mary stopped, not just at the mention of her name, but at the sound of the voice: it was distinctly male, rich, deep and beautiful.

She turned around and found herself standing before a man, a very tall man. She craned her neck to look up at him. His hair was the color of the sun and his skin as iridescent as jewels. He was dressed in a white robe and smiling at her. Unsettled by his appearance and the fact that he, a stranger, called her by name, Mary backed up against the well. *What kind of greeting is this*, Mary wondered? Was he trying to flatter her? What did he want?

"Fear not, Mary: for you have found favor with *Adonai*," the man reassured her.

She looked into his face. His features were…indescribable; he was neither Roman nor Jew. So, what then did that make him, especially with his talk of G-d?

"You will become pregnant and give birth to a son, and you will name him Jesus. He will be great and will be called the Son of the Highest: and the L-rd *Adonai* will give him the throne of his father David. And he will reign over the house of Jacob forever, and of his kingdom, there will be no end."

The words came out in a rush, filling Mary's head with images of deliverance and prophecy. Then the magnitude of the stranger's words dawned on her: she would be the mother of the *Mashiac*! The very thing she prayed about each morning was being fulfilled and she was being chosen as the vessel who would birth G-d's salvation. That was wondrous news, except…

"How can this be? I am still a virgin."

He smiled at her, sending a wave of comfort and assurance over her.

"The Holy Spirit will come on you, and the power of the Highest will overshadow you and the holy child born of you will be called the Son of *Adonai*," he said. There was a joyful mirth in his voice as he spoke. "For the things which are impossible with men are possible with *Adonai*. Remember your relative, Elizabeth, who was called barren? She is now six months pregnant, though she is past the age of childbearing."

Mary wasn't sure why, but her heart testified to the truth of the man's words and she glared up at him in building excitement. It had been sometime since Mary last saw Elizabeth, but her struggle to bear children was well known. Now she was finally going to be a mother! Such good news for her family and her people!

But the man was quiet now, a pensive look on his face; he seemed to wait on her. Then she understood why: though he had told her what would be, he was also asking her permission. It was her body the *Mashiac* would be born through—he needed her consent. G-d had never done anything that violated their freewill.

What of Joseph, though? What did this mean for him? Certainly if G-d was calling her, he was calling him as well. He wouldn't hesitate to give his consent. After all, they all prayed for the *Mashiac*; it would be his honor as much as hers.

There was only one thing to say then. Mary turned her gaze downward in a moment of reverence and said, "I am the L-rd's servant. May it happen to me as you have said."

Mary waited for a response but heard nothing. After a moment, she looked up and saw she was alone.

ANNA KNEADED THE dough, listening to the chatter of her younger daughters as they played on the floor beside her. There was once a day when she thought she would remain barren, like her sister Elizabeth, but G-d had blessed her with family. She placed the bread in a basket and tossed a warm cloth over it, so it could rise in time for dinner. Then she washed her hands in the bowl on the table and turned to her children.

"Can we eat now?" asked Kyra, the younger of the two.

Anna chuckled. It seemed the child rarely thought of anything but food.

"Come, let's wash up," she responded, taking her hand.

The door opened. Expecting Mary, Anna was surprised to see Heli and Nathan instead.

"Good morning, my love," Heli said. He took her by the waist and kissed her. Anna blushed as the girls giggled and Nathan groaned. "That's what I wanted to hear," he added, smiling at his children's responses. He released Anna to wash his hands, looked around and asked, "Where's Mary?"

"I don't know. I sent her for water, but she hasn't returned," Anna replied, now concerned. Sentries who marched through Nazareth were known to stop and question the locals at times.

"We haven't had any trouble with the Romans lately, but I'll go look for her," her husband said, trying to assuage her uncertainties, though it was apparent he felt the same. He dried his hands and started towards the door, when Mary entered, the water pot in her hands.

Relieved, Anna asked, "Where were you, child?"

Mary set the pot down and responded, "At the well, as you asked."

"Well, don't take so long next time," Anna advised, and ushered her family to the table. Everyone followed her lead, except Mary, who remained standing near the door. She seemed to want to say something else.

"What is it?" Anna asked.

"There was a man at the well," her daughter ventured.

"What man?" Heli interrupted. Anna heard the edge in his voice and knew he was ready to fight for his daughter's honor.

"He was a *malakh*. He said the *Mashiac* was coming and I would be his mother."

Silence fell over them. Anna glared at her daughter, unsure of what to think. Mary was never given to stories or wild imaginations, neither was she gullible, so what was this?

"A *malakh*?" Heli asked.

"He was very tall and brilliant, like the sun." Mary lifted her hand high above her head to illustrate her words.

"He said he was a *malakh*?"

"Well, no, but he couldn't have been anything else."

"And he said that you would be the mother of the *Mashiac*," Heli continued. "What about Joseph? Will he be the father?"

Mary shook her head and said, "The child will be from *Adonai*."

All became silent again, even the little ones. Anna looked at Nathan, Oprah and Kyra, who were waiting at the table for the situation to be resolved; they seemed to sense something wasn't right.

Anna closed the gap between them, Heli behind her.

"How will this be? How can you become pregnant without having relations with a man?" Her voice was considerably lower.

The mirth in Mary's eyes disappeared.

"He said the Holy Spirit will come on me and fill my womb with the son of *Adonai*," Mary responded, meekly.

"That is blasphemy, Mary," Heli advised, the edge back in his voice. He looked around, as though someone might hear them. "You are smart enough to know you ought not speak that way."

"But you taught us to pray," Mary pleaded, turning to Anna, "'I am available to you, *Adonai*...'"

Anna wanted to believe Mary. After all, this was her sensible, obedient child with a practical head on her shoulders. She had never been one for fantastic stories, so why was she telling them now? Did she not understand the implications of what she was embracing? Pregnant by the Holy Spirit? What would Joseph say? Or worse, his mother? If the woman found out, who would stop her from running to the priest? Mary would be stoned for adultery! Is that what G-d was asking of her? Of them? Anna would be guilty of disbelief if Mary was right, but G-d had been silent for so long, there was no way she could accept he had chosen her daughter, of all the maidens in Galilee, to bear the *Mashiac*?

"He even said *Doda* Elizabeth is with child," Mary added quietly.

Anna had her answer. Laughing, she responded, "Elizabeth is past her child-bearing years. She could no more have a child than your *abba* could. And if she was pregnant, then she would have sent word, so we could rejoice with her and you know we haven't heard from her. Really Mary, you can't be this naïve, trusting the words of a complete stranger. You're no longer a child, you're fourteen. You need to act like the woman you're expected to be. Now stop this nonsense and tell no one about it."

With that, Anna ended the conversation and went back to ushering her family to the table. Only the younger children followed, though. Heli remained standing, his eyes on Mary, whose face was downcast. The excitement was gone from her demeanor. It hurt Anna to deflate her mood, but she knew it was for the best.

15 *Nisan*

MARY WAS ATTENTIVE AS ANNA closed the morning prayer.

"So be it," Anna said.

"So be it," Mary, Oprah and Kyla repeated.

Without being told, Mary grabbed her veil and covered her head. Then she picked up the water jar and said, "I'll get the water, *imma*."

Anna nodded her head as Oprah and Kyla jumped up and down, vying for her attention. Though her mother was distracted this morning, Mary suspected Anna knew why she was so anxious to do her chores— she hoped to see the *malakh* at the well again. She had been obedient and not brought up the incident in the week since she saw him, but it had constantly been on her mind. And how could it not, when every morning she uttered the same prayer, 'I am available to you, *Adonai*, that I might be the mother of your *Mashiac*.' The prayer held new meaning for her: she was the Chosen One. G-d had regarded her, a lowly maiden, and favored her, promising to do a great work through her, much as he had done for her forefathers. And that was wonderful news...until Mary considered her parents' reactions. Then she began to doubt herself, doubt her senses. Perhaps she had imagined the whole incident, perhaps it was her overly active imagination. Maybe none of it was real.

It was this thought that had her rushing to the well but there was no *malakh* waiting on her, only Rachel, an older girl from town, who was as condescending as she was pretty—probably the only thing keeping her unwed.

"*Shalom,*" Rachel greeted her.

Mary forced a smile and replied, "*Shalom,* Rachel."

"I heard Joseph came by your house a couple of weeks ago."

"He brought me a gift," Mary said, as she placed her jar beside Rachel's.

"That's so precious," Rachel said. Mary detected sarcasm in her tone. "I had several suitors when I was your age and they often brought me gifts. All different kinds, perfumes, jewels, clothes—oh, one of them even brought me a silk cloth. Can you imagine? He said he had traded for it with a man from the Orient."

Mary smiled again, wanting to be polite.

"Of course, the suitors couldn't come up with a dowry, so my *abba* turned them away. That's alright; because I am more mature now and know those men would not have been good for me. I am waiting for the right one."

Like Joseph, Mary thought. Rachel had hoped he would court her, since they were the same age; and he was a handsome man. But Joseph chose Mary. And Rachel remained unmarried.

"How is your *imma*?" Rachel asked her.

"She is well. My sisters keep her busy," Mary responded.

"That's good. It's inspiring, you know, that she was able to find someone and bear children at her age. It offers hope to the rest of us."

"She's not so old," Mary insisted. True, her mother was older, but not as old as Rachel implied.

"Oh, of course not. I didn't mean to suggest that," Rachel stated, patting Mary's hand. "I was just saying she is blessed, that's all."

Rachel smiled innocently, but Mary knew otherwise.

"Well, let me get back before my *imma* worries. Oh, and be careful; I've heard there are strange men hanging around here."

And with that, Rachel picked up her water pot and headed home, leaving Mary to wonder what her admonition was supposed to mean. Romans? Rogues? The *malakh*? Mary sighed and decided she didn't really want to know.

18 *Nisan*

WITH A FINAL TUG, MARY TIGHTENED the stitch and cut the thread loose. Though she was not finished yet, she held the dress up for inspection. It was white and simple but once she decorated it with ornate beads and lavish embroidery, it would be beautiful. After all, a bride had to look her best on the day of her *nissuin*.

Anna dropped into the chair beside her and picked up the dress she had been mending. She put one stitch into it before letting it fall into her lap.

"Children are a blessing, Mary, don't ever forget that. But they will wear you out. Those two girls have so much energy, it is a wonder they were able to go down for a nap," Anna sighed. She closed her eyes and rested her head back.

Mary stopped sewing and glanced at her, still thinking about Rachel's comments. So what if she had a few wrinkles on her face and some grey hairs weaving in and out of her curly black tresses? They were a testament to all that she had gone through. If anything, she was beautiful.

"*Imma,*" Mary said, placing her dress gently on her lap. "Why does *Adonai* make some women barren and others fertile?"

Anna sat up. She took a deep breath and said, "Honestly, Mary, I don't know. Sometimes it's what he wills. And then sometimes he removes the curse so that we can fulfill our purpose." She paused for a moment and added, "I thought for the longest time I would be cursed, but *Adonai* filled my house instead."

"So some are chosen and others not…," Mary stated, pulling on a stray thread.

Anna nodded her head.

"We can only abide by his will and pray for understanding," Anna said. "Why do you ask? Do you worry you won't be able to give Joseph children?"

"I was just…thinking…," Mary stammered. "…about something Rachel said about you when I saw her at the well," There was no guile in her response, but she couldn't speak the absolute truth either—that she was still thinking of the *malakh,* about *Doda* Elizabeth, about becoming the mother of the *Mashiac.*

Anna studied her carefully, as if trying to determine how to answer her. She finally sighed and picked up the dress.

"Just ignore that girl. She's let her bitterness infect her like a disease and now she runs around trying to infect others," Anna said simply and returned to the task at hand.

Mary said nothing more. She put the thoughts out of her mind and decided that maybe her mother was right. Why would G-d choose her? Out of all the maidens in Israel? Who was she to deserve such an honor?

Still, there was a part of her that desperately wanted what the *malakh* had told her to be true. It would mean that G-d saw her, saw her family, saw her people. It would mean that he had not forgotten them. And to be honest, the idea of being chosen by G-d himself…well, who wouldn't want that?

Mary sighed and shook her head. The *malakh* had not returned, but if G-d had spoken through him, his words would prove true in time. And if not, then her mother's words would prove correct. Either way, Mary had a dress to finish.

25 *Nisan*

A WARM BREEZE BLEW THROUGH THE yard. Mary closed her eyes and tilted her head back, enjoying the sun as it warmed her face. She opened her eyes again and looked up at the sky overhead, birds flying around in search of their next meal. All was quiet for the moment. Then laughter erupted, as her sisters ran around, chasing each other. Their ample energy had earned them an early playtime outside so Anna could clean up their mess inside, which left Mary to keep an eye on them. She watched as Kyla snuck up on Oprah and tagged her. Oprah turned and chased her. Kyla ran to Mary and grabbed her dress, turning her around so Oprah couldn't catch her. Oprah managed to get her arms around Mary and touch Kyla, both of them giggling. Mary smiled; she loved to hear their laughter.

"I got you," Oprah cried and ran off.

Kyla smiled and ran after her. She stopped in mid-stride though when she saw

Oprah coming back towards her. She ran to Mary and grabbed her hand, pulling her along. Mary's veil flew off her head as they ran in the opposite direction. She let it fall to the ground and continued to play with her sisters, chasing them around the yard as if she were one of them.

"Mary!"

The girls came to an abrupt stop as they realized Miriam, Joseph's mother, was watching them, a look of disapproval on her face. Mary straightened up her posture and faced the woman. She was a large woman, not much older than Anna, but her hair was grey, and her face permanently creased. Mary couldn't recall ever seeing the woman smile and felt uncomfortable under her stern gaze.

"Where is your veil?" Miriam asked.

Mary lifted her hand to her head and smoothed out her hair. She dared a glance behind her, where the veil lay on the ground. Turning back to Miriam, she open-ed her mouth to respond, but was cut off.

"What will others think, you running around like a common woman?"

Mary looked down under the weight of the chastisement.

"Where is your mother?"

"Miriam."

Mary raised her head to see her mother approaching them.

"Where is your daughter's veil? Is this how you let her behave?" Miriam stated indignantly.

"Mary was helping me with the little ones. I'm sure it just fell from her head," Anna responded coolly.

"Well, she should have stopped to cover her head. It is her glory."

"I'm sure she was going to do that," Anna stated, shooting Mary a pointed look before leading Miriam towards the house. "Come on in."

Unmoved by the comment, Miriam gave Mary one last look of condemnation before following Anna inside. Mary sighed and walked over to her veil. Oprah and Kyla approached her as she picked it up and placed it back on her head.

"Are you in trouble for playing with us?" Oprah asked quietly.

Mary heard the concern in her sister's voice and smiled.

"No, I'm not. Come on, let's go play something else."

1 *Iyar*

MARY SAT UP ON HER MAT. IT WAS still dark outside; however, she couldn't sleep any more, unlike her brother and sisters. Their slumber was deep and unaffected by the concerns of the world…concerns that were robbing Mary of sleep: her menstrual cycle was late and there was no indication it was coming.

And why should there be, she chastised herself. Isn't that what the *malakh* said?

She sighed and lay back down, pulling her blanket up to her chin. Its smell and familiarity were comforting, yet not enough to give her peace. This was supposed to be a time of celebration. Their long-awaited savior was coming. G-d had heard them and had answered their prayers. He had chosen her and honored her. Yet all she could do was worry. Her parents had insisted she not speak of the incident, and all the while, Joseph remained oblivious of what was to be their destiny, their glory. What was she supposed to do?

Mary pulled the blanket over her head. She had to talk to her parents. And Joseph, especially Joseph. The longer she waited, the harder it would be for him. Would he believe she had not been faithful? Surely, he wouldn't. He had to know she cared for him and would never do that.

She sat up again, frustration abounding. She should have told him the same day.

She sighed once more. It was too late to lament that now.

Mary lay back down again. All she could do now was talk to her parents and move forward.

She listened as Kyla snored, Oprah turned over on her mat and Nathan mumbled something in his sleep—all while she was wide awake. Yes, the sooner she talked to her parents, the better.

3 *Iyar*

"MARY."

Lost in her thoughts, Mary didn't hear her mother calling her. She was tired. Or weary. Or just frustrated. It had been three days and she still hadn't found the right words to communicate with her parents. Every time she tried, her stomach twisted into knots and her heart beat loudly…like she was guilty of wrongdoing.

"Mary."

But she had done nothing wrong, so why did she feel this way?

Because her parents didn't believe her. And perhaps they had reason not to—G-d had been silent for so long. Why would he choose to speak now? And to her, of all people? Mary had no answer, but regardless of her diminutive state, she couldn't deny the fact that she was with child while still a virgin. This was something only G-d could do.

"Mary, pray!" Anna stated.

Hearing the exasperated tone in her mother's voice, Mary straightened up. She was supposed to be praying, uttering the same words she said every morning. *I am available to you, Adonai, that I might be the mother of your Mashiac.* But she already was his mother. Or she would be in eight months. So what was she supposed to say?

"What's wrong?" Anna asked, the concern in her voice obvious. "You've been acting strange for days and now you're not praying?"

"I'm sorry, *Imma*," Mary said, as her stomach began twisting into the ever-familiar knots. She dropped her gaze and cleared her throat. "*Adonai*, I am available to you…" Mary's heart raced. Did she say what she always said? Or did she tell her mother what she didn't want to hear? "I am available to you, and I thank you…for choosing me to be the mother of your *Mashiac*."

ANNA GLARED AT her oldest child, incredulously.

"What did you say?"

Mary didn't respond, nor did she raise her head.

"Mary," Anna warned.

Quietly, her daughter replied, "'Thank you for choosing me to be the mother of your *Mashiac*.'"

Anna took in a deep breath. She had hoped their last conversation on the subject was the end of the matter, but apparently it wasn't. She turned to Oprah and Kyla.

"Girls, go and wait for me in your room."

Oprah stood up, but Kyla objected, "I'm hungry."

Anna got up and escorted the girls to their room.

"Shortly. Just go for now."

The girls obeyed. Anna turned back to Mary.

"Look at me," she said.

Mary met her eyes. Anna saw no rebellion, just determination.

"I know…," Anna began, softening her tone. "I know you want to believe you saw a *malakh*—"

Mary interrupted, "But I did!"

"Why would *Adonai* send a *malakh* to you? Why would he choose you?" Anna insisted. She knew her tone was harsh, but she needed to get her point across to Mary. "Be practical about this. It's admirable that you desire to serve *Adonai*, but this…this is a death sentence. You need to let this go and never speak of it again."

Mary picked at a loose thread on her sleeve and said nothing.

"It is settled then," Anna stated, ready to call her girls back in, until Mary said, "I am with child."

Her words were so abrupt that they felt like a knife tearing into Anna's heart. Unwilling to believe she heard her correctly, Anna exclaimed, "What?"

Mary looked back up at her. The determination was gone from her eyes, leaving only fear.

"I am with child," she repeated, her voice so low Anna had to strain to hear her.

Stunned, Anna dropped into the chair across from Mary. She looked at her daughter: long dark hair, piercing black eyes, beautiful olive skin. Anna recalled the joy and hope she felt when she first held her. Now it was all being torn from her.

"My cycle is late," Mary added.

Grasping for hope, Anna said, "Well, it can still come."

Mary shook her head.

"So, then you...and Joseph—" Anna began but was interrupted by Mary, who exclaimed, "No! Joseph and I haven't…we haven't been intimate."

"Then you and another boy?"

"I told you. The *malakh* said I would bear the *Mashiac*. I would become pregnant by the Holy One."

"But that is impossible," Anna insisted, raising her voice. She stood up and walked over to her work table, leaning on it for support. "That is impossible," she repeated before turning back to her daughter.

Mary shook her head. Her lips were trembling, and she was crying now. Anna wanted to pull her into her arms and comfort her, to wipe away her tears, erase everything that had been said…but she couldn't. Between the fear creeping up in her and the anger that Mary would do something like this, Anna was stuck, frozen where she stood.

"Mary, tell me the truth," she said with a steady voice. "Who is the father? Who are you protecting? Were you not happy with Joseph? Was he not agreeable to you?"

Mary said nothing, wiping her tears.

"Mary—"

"I told you. This child is of *Adonai*. I haven't been with any man."

Anna heard the conviction in her voice and knew Mary was not lying. But that wasn't possible, it just wasn't possible.

THE HOUSE WAS unusually quiet. At one time, Heli would have relished the silence, but that morning it was agonizing. It had been one hour since he and Nathan arrived home from the synagogue, one hour since Mary revealed her condition, one hour since their lives changed. With the children waiting in their room, he and Anna now had to consider what to do. But Heli found it difficult to put two thoughts together, much less grasp the reality of the moment: his Mary, pregnant?

"This is unlike her," he stated, more to himself.

Anna paced the floor, as she had been doing for the past half-hour.

"That's what I don't understand. She just isn't the type to sneak around. She seemed to genuinely care for Joseph. Why this? Why now?"

Heli heard the desperation in her voice, but he didn't respond…at least not with the answer she wanted to hear.

"What if she's telling the truth?" he asked.

"That's just not possible," Anna insist-ed.

"But it was prophesied."

"*Adonai* has not spoken to his people in four hundred years. Is this how he does it now? By condemning a young, innocent woman to death? Who will believe her? Joseph? That mother of his? Will they believe *Adonai* did this or that she was unfaithful? You know what they will do: they'll stone her to death."

Anna tried to keep her composure, but it was too much. One tear escaped, then another, until they were streaming down her face and her lips were trembling. Heli stood up from the table and took his wife into his arms. She was not normally so emotional, neither was she cynical, but he understood why she was behaving as she did: Mary was their miracle, the child Barren Anna was never supposed to have. He knew about the jeers and spiteful words she had to endure when they were first married. To lose Mary now would be to bring back all those memories. What could they do, though?

As if Anna could read his mind, she pulled away from his embrace and said, "We have to send her away before she begins to show."

Releasing her completely, he asked, "What?"

"We have to send her away before she starts showing," she reiterated.

Heli found his way to his chair, exhausted and hungry. He sighed.

"Where are we going to send her?"

Anna was suddenly energized, and Heli feared she was just grasping at false hope now.

"To my sister, in Hebron. Mary was a small child last time she was there. They won't remember her."

Heli shook his head. While there was some merit to her idea, there was one detail Anna was forgetting: "Her husband is a priest. Do you really think he will disregard the law for family?"

"It doesn't matter, he's gone senile," Anna replied. "I heard he was serving in the temple in Jerusalem last *Elul*, when he was struck deaf and dumb. He does not speak, cannot hear and no longer travels to Jerusalem to serve. He is senile. He will pose no problem for Mary."

Heli sadly considered the fate that had befallen his brother-in-law—a fate that now served them.

"So, we send her to Elizabeth. What then? What do we tell Joseph?" he asked, shaking his head.

"We tell him the truth—she went to her *doda*'s home. The day of their *nissuin* is still some time away."

"But for how long? And what about the child?" Heli continued. He knew where her thought process was going, knew they were about to tread on lies. If they went there, there was no turning back. "Anna, think this through," he pleaded with her. "What happens when Mary returns? Will she hide the truth from Joseph? Will he marry her under false pretenses? Will there be blood on the night of her *nissuin* to show she is a virgin?"

Anna remained determined, almost defiant, and said, "I will not lose my daughter."

Heli knew there was no arguing with her. He took a deep breath and said, "Alright."

10 *Iyar*

WITH QUIET RESIGNATION, MARY folded her other dress and carefully packed it into her personal basket. She handled the bird Joseph had carved for her carefully, and packed it alongside her belongings. Her *abba* gathered provisions for the trip and her *imma* selected gifts for her aunt. The once mirthful Oprah and Kyra sat quietly by the door, playing with their dolls, the joy that filled the house earlier gone with Mary's announcement a week prior.

Mary sighed and sat back down on her bed. Her eyes stung with each tear she shed. She didn't want to go to Hebron, but the fact that her parents wouldn't let her see Joseph hurt more. They didn't trust her. And worse than that, they expected her to just obey. She was to go to her *doda's* house, have her child, come back as though nothing happened and let her 'pious aunt' raise the babe.

Heli entered the room. Mary wiped the tears from her face.

"Are you ready?" he asked. His voice was low and there were bags under his eyes, as if he had not been sleeping.

"Don't make me go, *abba*," she begged.

Heli sat beside her and maintained eye contact with her.

"You understand why we're doing this, don't you?"

"But I did nothing wrong," she insisted.

He looked down but didn't say anything. A single tear ran down his face as he took her hands in his.

"Mary, please tell me," he begged, straining to keep his voice steady. "Tell me…is Joseph the father?"

She slowly pulled her hands out of his, reminded how neither he, nor her mother, believed her.

"Mary…," her *abba* began, but there was nothing else to say. Heli rose from the bed and murmured, "Let's go."

Resigned to her fate, Mary followed.

11 *Iyar*

THE NIGHT AIR WAS CHILLY BUT better than the day's heat, Joseph decided. Sitting on the roof of his home, he stretched out and turned his gaze to the stars above him. It was a moonless night, and the stars offered their own light, twinkling brightly against the dark backdrop. Joseph sighed, enjoying the moment and the way it reminded him of Mary—her beautiful, round face; her intense, black eyes; her flowing, long hair…

Joseph took a deep breath and let it out slowly. He wasn't ready to bring Mary home as his wife, so he couldn't entertain impure thoughts.

He took another deep breath and turned his mind back to the moment. No, to his work: another table with chairs for the miller. His family was growing, fast; and two of his sons were already following in their father's work. Joseph smiled; one day he and Mary would have a son who would become a carpenter, just like him…

And with that, his thoughts were back to Mary: she seemed distracted last time he saw her. Maybe she was ill, or tired; she did help her mother carry the weight of the household. He would have to check on her.

Joseph beamed at the thought.

13 *Iyar*

THE NIGHT AIR WAS CHILLY BUT better than the day's heat, Mary decided. After traveling for two days under the scorching sun, the cool temperature was comforting.

Mary sat down in front of the campfire, listening as Joanna, the wife of the caravan leader, quietly sang to her son, lulling him to sleep. Mary's father had paid them to take her to Hebron. There was safety in numbers and though there was always a threat from highwaymen or Romans, even in a group, this was a better alternative to traveling alone, especially for a fourteen-year-old girl.

Woman, Mary corrected herself. She was now a woman—a betrothed, pregnant woman.

She sighed and turned away from the scene in front of her. This was the last thing she wanted to think about right now. She had to find something else to focus on.

She would arrive at the home of her *doda* and *dod* the next day, she could think about that. It had been years since she last saw them. Mary remembered seeing her uncle perform the temple rites at the local synagogue. She recalled the peace that filled their home, though there was always sorrow that they never had children of their own. It hurt Mary's heart to think of her mother's plan, but perhaps it was no coincidence that she was heading to their home. The *malakh* had mentioned Elizabeth, and if his words for Mary had come to pass, then certainly his words about Elizabeth had proven true as well. Which meant if anyone was to believe Mary's tale of meeting the *malakh* and becoming the mother of the *Mashiac*, it would be her. And maybe, because of that, she could provide a different perspective than that of her parents, a perspective that could help Mary.

Comforted by the thought, Mary turned back to the fire and settled in to sleep.

14 *Iyar*

ELIZABETH WIPED THE SWEAT FROM her brow and looked down at the progress she had made. Her garden was small but big enough to provide for her and Zechariah.

And our son, she considered with a smile. She placed her hand on her growing belly, barely able to contain the excitement welling up in her. In two months, she would be a mother!

"*Adonai*, you are great," she said and decided it was time to go inside. Elizabeth rose slowly, resting her weight on her knees. She protectively wrapped her hand around her midsection as she stood to her full height and stretched out her back. Then she waddled into the house and found her way to her work table, where she washed her hands. A quiet voice interrupted her thoughts.

"*Doda*."

A shiver ran down Elizabeth's spine. Before she could even turn around to greet her guest, the child within her womb began to leap and turn, so much so she had to stop and catch her breath. He had never moved like this, but then this was different, wasn't it? The visitor was special, and Elizabeth knew it in her spirit.

She turned toward the door to see a young woman with long, black hair and piercing, dark eyes.

Mary.

There was uncertainty in her stance, but Elizabeth saw beyond it to that which was in her: her strength, her practicality, her love. More than that, though, Elizabeth was taken with the grace and favor that covered her— her and the child within her. Elizabeth didn't know how she knew, but she did. Joy suddenly filled her.

"Imagine, the mother of my L-rd in my home!" she stated and gathered Mary up in her arms. "You are blessed among women and blessed…" –Elizabeth pulled back from her and cupped her face – "…is the fruit of your womb."

She took in Mary's hopeful expression and laughed.

"You know, when the sound of your greeting reached my ears, the baby leaped for joy inside me!" Elizabeth laughed again. "Oh, my dear, you are blessed, don't you know? Because you believed, you are blessed; and now you will see fulfilled what *Adonai* has spoken. Just wait."

MARY SMILED. ELIZABETH knew, and she didn't even have to tell her. Mary felt as if a weight had been taken off her shoulders, and at that moment, she allowed the emotions to burst forth from her heart.

"I await his fulfillment," she began, "The breath of my being made great the name of the L-rd, and his joy expands within me, his handmaiden. Because he has made his favor obvious, people from all ages will say I have attained the blessing of the heavens and they will make my name supreme because *Adonai*'s name is sacred. His words persist through the ages to those who fear him. He has scattered the proud and toppled the mighty from their thrones. He has exalted the lowly and satisfied the hungry with good things, though he sends the rich away empty. *Adonai* has helped Israel, just as he spoke to Abraham and his descendants, and fulfilled his promise for the *Mashiac* through me."

Mary embraced Elizabeth again and hung onto her tightly, happy to have an ally. Then she felt a jab to her midsection and remembered Elizabeth's pregnancy. She pulled away and looked down at her *doda's* belly, protruding greatly in front of her. Mary laughed, realizing the child kicked her. She let her hands slide down Elizabeth's arm to her bulging womb.

"*Adonai* is great, is he not?" Elizabeth said, her voice filled with awe and wonder.

"I had almost forgotten." Mary turned her gaze up. Elizabeth was older than Anna and the years showed. Her hair was streaked with gray and she had wrinkles on her face; yet it shined like that of a young woman, with a smile that lit up the room.

"I can't help but marvel at the goodness of *Adonai*," Elizabeth laughed, placing her hand on her belly. "They called me barren, but now I am going to be a mother."

Mary beamed, happy to be a part of her aunt's joy.

"Oh, but listen to me go on and on like an old cow," Elizabeth said. "Look at you. You've grown up to be a beautiful young woman. And favored too. Surely your *abba* and *imma* are proud. There must be an *iyshah* now, too, right? Where are they?"

Mary stopped and looked down. For a brief, wonderful moment, she had forgotten she would have to explain her presence there.

"You know what?" Elizabeth said, softening her tone. Mary turned back to her and could see the understanding in her eyes. "Let's get you settled in. I'm sure you're tired after the trip. Come."

Mary nodded, gratefully.

15 *Iyar*

THE SUN STREAMED IN THROUGH THE window onto Mary. She opened her eyes, feeling the warmth on her face. She looked around briefly, confused: the room she shared with her brother and sisters had no window…

This isn't your room, that's why, she reminded herself, and closed her eyes, remembering now she was in Elizabeth's house. This was to be her home for the better part of the next year. Mary had explained everything to her aunt the previous evening, anxious to get it out of her heart. In response, Elizabeth simply offered her a warm smile and told her everything would work out the way *Adonai* had intended.

With a sigh, Mary rose from her bed and got ready. Her stomach growled—between the anxiety and the traveling, she had barely eaten in the past week. But her appetite was back now. She made her way downstairs, expecting to find the hustle and bustle she was accustomed to with three younger siblings, but there was none. The house was quiet, and she was alone.

Mary looked around. The place was bigger than her home. Her uncle was not wealthy, but as a priest, he was taken care of. He was blessed and that counted more.

Mary peered into her aunt and uncle's room, but it was empty. She went outside and walked around the house to the back, where she found Elizabeth sitting in her garden, pulling up weeds. Elizabeth looked up as she approached and smiled.

"How did you sleep, my dear?" she asked.

Mary took a seat beside her and replied, "Good, though you should have woken me up earlier. I never sleep this late."

"You were tired. You need your rest now more than ever," Elizabeth gently reminded her. "Have you eaten? I left a plate for you on the table."

"No, not yet."

"Well, come on," Elizabeth said, reaching for her. Mary allowed the older woman to lean on her while she rose to her feet. Her belly seemed bigger now that she was standing above her, and Mary couldn't help but stare. Is this what she would look like in a few months' time?

"Are you coming?"

Mary met her gaze and realized she was not paying attention. She stood up and followed Elizabeth into the house. She sat down at the table, while her aunt poured her a cup of milk. She noted her uncle's absence and asked, "Where is *Dod* Zechariah?"

Elizabeth sat down across from her and offered her a tired smile.

"At the synagogue."

"*Imma* said he was senile."

Elizabeth chuckled and sat back, her arms resting on her belly.

"It's good to know the gossip circles are still going strong. Your mother knows better than to believe everything she hears." The humor in her voice had not faded, but there was something of a reproach in her words.

"Is that why you didn't say anything about being with child?" Mary asked, the food on her plate still untouched. Elizabeth pointed to it and said, "I'll answer your questions, just eat. I don't want to send you back to your mother, emaciated."

Mary obeyed.

Satisfied, her aunt stated, "Now, let's start with your uncle…"

ELIZABETH SMILED WITH fond recollection. Her *iyshah*, Zechariah.

"I wish you had known him when he was younger. He was quite the romantic. He would bring me fresh flowers from the field whenever he came to see me. He would tell me stories about the heroes of old and share how he knew that *Adonai* had not abandoned his people and had greatness planned for us. He was a young man, full of faith—a faith that did not dissipate even when we married, and it became obvious I could not conceive. He prayed and brought offerings to *Adonai* and waited. Still I remained barren. It was as if *Adonai* stopped listening. I don't think Zechariah ever stopped praying—for the people he ministered to, for the land, for our lost brethren—but I do think part of him stopped praying for us."

She paused, the fond look lost to sorrow.

"There are moments, Mary, when you will doubt *Adonai* is still listening or that you even heard him correctly. But don't ever doubt that he is real, because he is. And he does hear you; and just like he did our forefathers, he will surprise you.

"Your uncle's lot to serve fell on the Festival of Tabernacles last year. As he had done for many years, he traveled to

Jerusalem and got ready. Dressed in the robe of the ephod, he tied a robe around him and entered the Holy of Holies, where he lit the incense, as the worshippers prayed outside. Then a *malakh* appeared beside the altar. Zechariah immediately became fearful, thinking perhaps he had sinned before *Adonai* and not accounted for it. But the messenger comforted him and said, 'Fear not, Zechariah: for *Adonai* has heard your prayer'. Imagine, Mary, *Adonai* heard his prayers: the ones he offered for the people and the ones he offered for me, years and years ago.

"Then the *malahk* said, 'Your wife Elizabeth shall bear you a son, and you will call his name John. You will have joy and gladness; and many will rejoice at his birth. For he will be great in the sight of the L-rd and will drink neither wine nor strong drink; and he will be filled with the Holy Spirit, even from his mother's womb. And many of the children of Israel will he turn to the L-rd their G-d. And he will go before him in the spirit and power of Elijah, to turn the hearts of the fathers to the children, and the disobedient to the wisdom of the just; to make ready a people prepared for the L-rd.'"

Elizabeth stopped again. As wonderful as it was retelling the story, it pained her to remember the next part. She furrowed her brows and continued with a little less enthusiasm than she started with.

"You have to understand, Zechariah had prayed for a long time without response and I had ceased my monthly flow. It seemed as if *Adonai* had forsaken us, but I suppose there's never any good reason for doubting *Adonai*'s word.

"Zechariah asked the *malakh* how he would know this. The man answered, 'I am Gabriel, who stands in the presence of *Adonai*; I have been sent to speak to you to give you this good news. But because you do not believe me, you will be mute and deaf until the day these things happen.' And that's what occurred.

"Well, you can imagine the people waiting for Zechariah became worried. Were they actually going to have to pull him out? Had he committed some egregious sin and been struck dead?" –Elizabeth chuckled– "You know how people are, always in need of something to talk about and Zechariah gave them that when he came out of the Holy of Holies unable to speak or hear. Some said he had seen a miracle, but others simply chose to believe he had gone senile.

"He finished up his week and came home. He couldn't tell me what happened, but he wrote down what he could and left the rest to *Adonai*. I think that's the moment when my faith came back to life. I wanted everything he said, and I set my heart to it. And when I found out I was with child, it was the happiest moment of my life, of *our* lives."

"Why didn't you send word then?" Mary interrupted.

"What did your mother say when you told her?"

Mary didn't respond, her face betraying the turmoil of emotion inside her. Still Elizabeth knew.

"She didn't believe you, right?" she offered.

Mary nodded, sadly.

"It's alright. I don't begrudge her. Sometimes we just have to shut out the gossipers and let our faith overtake us. *Adonai* will fill us with enough grace to deal with the naysayers so that when the time is right, they will have no choice but to believe. That's why I said nothing and stayed hidden; I knew no one would believe without evidence. Does that make sense?"

"Yes, *doda*."

Elizabeth patted her niece's hand. "I've told you enough stories for now. Finish eating."

Mary dutifully obeyed.

17 *Iyar*

JOSEPH MADE HIS WAY DOWN THE path to Mary's house, located on the edge of town. The walk wasn't long, perhaps fifteen minutes, but he was sweaty and covered in sawdust. He should've washed up and changed; however, he really wanted to see Mary.

He wiped his forehead with his sleeve and took the steps down the alley, clutching the flowers in his other hand, flowers he had picked for Mary on his way there. They weren't much, but they gave him a reason to see her.

Joseph turned the corner and saw Mary's house. He bounded the last few steps and with the flowers behind his back, he knocked on the door, trying to be patient. He began to knock again, when the door opened. Heli stood there, a look of surprise on his face.

"Joseph!" he exclaimed. "How are you?"

Joseph smiled; he liked the older man. In his own way, he reminded Joseph of his father, Jacob, who had passed away several years earlier. With his father gone from this world, Joseph was left with a void. Now that he was betrothed and getting ready to become a husband, and one day a father, Joseph couldn't help but think himself fortunate that he should be able to call Heli his father-in-law.

"I am well, thank you," he replied.

"How is your *imma*?" Heli asked.

"She is also well."

"Good, good."

Joseph paused, waiting for Heli to continue, but an awkward silence followed instead. He expected to hear the younger children screaming or running around like they always did, but not a sound could be heard from inside the house. Joseph cleared his throat and asked, "Is Mary here?"

"No," Heli responded, looking back into the house, then out at him. "She is not here. She is visiting family in the hill country."

Joseph tried not to sound disappointed.

"When will she return?"

"Ah…well, it's a delicate situation …with the kinsman, you see…she could be gone for months."

"Oh," Joseph said, not even trying to mask his emotions this time.

"I'm sorry. We should have sent word, but it's just busy here, with the little ones."

Taking in a deep breath, Joseph said, "No, I understand."

Heli patted him on the shoulder.

"You're a good man."

Joseph offered him a weak smile in response.

"I'll tell Anna you stopped by," Heli added as he shut the door, leaving Joseph in the doorway, holding the flowers he had brought for his betrothed. He looked down at them, wondering what to do now that Mary was gone.

She'll only be gone for a few months, he told himself. *She'll be back. It will give you time to make preparations so you can bring her home as your ishah.*

Though it was true, it didn't take away the disappointment of not seeing Mary.

She'll be back, Joseph told himself again and headed home.

20 *Iyar*

WITH HER HEAD COVERED AND EYES down, Mary followed her *doda* into the synagogue. Because her family had made the trek to Jerusalem once a year for the Passover Festival to worship in the Temple, Mary was familiar with the order of the house: women were allowed inside but were separated from the men, so as not to distract them from their devotion to G-d.

Elizabeth made her way through the halls into an overflow room in the back of the sanctuary. Mary followed her aunt, noting how small, dim and stuffy the room was. There was a buzz of conversation in there and several women stared at them as they entered, but mostly, the chatter continued. A woman, sharing the same facial features as them, approached and took Elizabeth into her arms.

"How are you feeling?"

Elizabeth laid her hand on her belly.

"Big, but well," she said with a chuckle and deliberately motioned to Mary. "Rona, you remember Mary, don't you?"

"Anna's Mary?" Rona asked, astonished. She looked her up and down, before hugging her as well. "You've grown up."

Mary blushed.

"She's expecting her first child," Elizabeth added.

Mary gave her a cautious look, but her aunt only offered her a 'don't worry' smile.

"That's wonderful!" Rona exclaimed. "And your husband?"

Before Mary could even begin to work on an excuse for her situation, Elizabeth confidently stated, "He's back in Nazareth. Mary is staying with me for a short time, so I can teach her and prepare her for child-birth."

Rona raised an eyebrow.

"Aren't you getting ahead of yourself? You've not had your first child yet."

"I raised you, didn't I, *bat-doda*?"

Rona put her arm around Mary. "She likes to think she did. In fact, she'd take credit for raising most of the young ones here in the hill country if we let her." Rona steered Mary towards the wall of women, facing the latticed framework that separated them from the main room, where the men were located.

Elizabeth followed them, saying, "Stop telling the girl lies, especially in the house of *Adonai.*"

Rona didn't acknowledge her, but quietly added, "You couldn't have a better teacher but don't tell her I said that."

Mary walked with her through the crowd and found a spot near the front. Silence fell over the room, as the priest started lighting the incense. Mary recognized the man as her uncle, Zechariah. She hadn't seen much of him since arriving in Hebron, but the glimpses she did catch were of an old man, hunched over scrolls, praying and seeking redemption. Now, he was absorbed in his task with an energy that betrayed his earlier stature. Mary turned to Elizabeth and noted the tenderness on her face as she watched her husband. Her love for him was obvious and Mary's face warmed at the thought of having caught her *doda* in an intimate moment. She brought her attention back to the front and listened as the men began their prayers.

1 *Sivan*

ELIZABETH TOOK A BREAK FROM washing clothes to stretch out and enjoy the cool breeze. The work was back-breaking enough without the babe kicking her. It seemed he couldn't wait to be born. Truth be told, she couldn't wait to meet him and hold him and introduce him to Zechariah and Mary and…

Speaking of which, where was Mary?

Elizabeth looked around her. Wading just at the river's edge was a handful of other women, chatting and washing clothes, but Mary was not amongst them. With a sigh, Elizabeth stood up and waddled up the path to her house. It was quiet, as always. Zechariah, she knew, was studying, but Mary was not in the main room, eating, as Elizabeth thought she might be. She found her, instead, in her room, lying down on her bed with her back to the door. The sun streaming in through the window illuminated her small figure.

"Are we going to rest all day?" Elizabeth asked, keeping her tone light so Mary knew she was not chiding her.

Mary rolled over and looked at her for a moment, before turning back to the wall. Elizabeth noted how red and swollen her eyes were. She walked over to Mary.

"What's wrong?"

Mary shook her head. Elizabeth uneasily lowered herself onto the bed, unable to find a comfortable spot. She ignored her body for a moment and turned her attention to Mary, wiping a tear as it fell from her eye.

"Tell me what's wrong, child," she softly pleaded. She had always felt a motherly connection to her sister's children. And even now, with Mary being as old as she was, expecting her first child, the sentiment was no different. "Are you ill?"

"No more than usual," Mary quietly stated. She had excused herself from dinner the previous evening after throwing up the contents of her stomach. Elizabeth knew she was embarrassed, but it was all part of the process: the child within her was growing and her body was making the necessary adjustments. Still, it had to be hard on her, being so young and away from home.

"Talk to me, *nechadnit*," Elizabeth said.

Mary lay back on the mat.

"*Doda*, I am grateful you've opened your home to me, but I'm supposed to be in Nazareth, getting ready for Joseph, not hiding from him. I'm supposed to be celebrating this pregnancy, enjoying the blessings and honor *Adonai* has bestowed on me, not hiding them from the world. Everything is so out of order; this is just not the way things are supposed to be."

The hurt in her voice was apparent. Elizabeth desired to be sensitive to her, but she knew Mary was still young. She still had some growing up and learning to do. Wisdom would come with age; until then, Mary would have to rely on the understanding of others to help her, which was where Elizabeth came in: she couldn't take the pain, but she could certainly offer wisdom.

"Life is not always as we think it should be. Look at our history: since the days of Abraham, many have tried to annihilate our people. Even as *Adonai*'s chosen, we are subjected to a cruel master. But we are still here. We are still multiplying, despite our people dying at the hands of the *goyem*. This is what it means to be favored and graced of *Adonai*. Not that life is supposed to be a certain way, but rather that his strength and his mercy are available to us for our survival. Look at me. I am still here. And because I am still here, I have lived to see the day when the stigma of barrenness was removed from me. This child will be a blessing to us and to the world. It is because of the grace of *Adonai* that we've survived long enough to see this day and now we can praise him for it. Do you understand what I am saying?"

Mary nodded.

"I know this situation is not ideal, but there is no precedent for it either. We can't say, this is how it should be. However, we can decide, with *Adonai*'s grace, to live long enough to see the end of what he started. You believed, now see it through," Elizabeth finished with a smile. Her heart always soared when it came to the things of G-d. She could talk about him forever.

Mary's countenance didn't change though.

"Your parents were doing what they thought was best for you," Elizabeth added, hoping to lift her spirit. "They love you. They were just trying to protect you."

Mary shrugged her shoulders.

"Tell you what; we'll write to your *imma*; perhaps she'll listen to reason. But it is *Adonai* you must put your faith in. He is the only one who can fix this, alright?"

Mary nodded in agreement.

"Good. Now help me up, we have clothes to wash."

12 *Sivan*

ANNA BALANCED THE JUG ON HER HIP, as Kyla and Oprah ran ahead of her. Getting water from the well often proved challenging, as the girls either ran off or got into a fight, causing her to momentarily abandon her task to deal with them. Today wasn't so bad, though, and Anna was thankful.

Oprah ran ahead, leaving Kyla behind her. The younger girl tried to keep up, but her little legs could only carry her so far. She stopped and turned back to her mother with tears in her eyes. Anna was glad for a break and set the jar down so she could pick her up. Kyla wrapped her arms around her. Anna felt the wet, warm tears trickle down her neck and couldn't help but feel hurt for her.

"Did Oprah leave you all alone?"

Kyla nodded her head.

Anna rubbed her daughter's back, remembering when she was the younger sister, running after Elizabeth the way Kyla ran after Oprah. It seemed the cycle never ended.

She turned Kyla's face to hers, peering into her teary, black eyes.

"Let's get home before your *abba* and *achichem* get there and you can help me make sweet bread."

Kyla's face brightened up just momentarily, before she asked, "And not Oprah?"

Anna laughed.

"This time it will be just you and me, okay?"

"Okay," Kyla agreed and wiped her face with the back of her hand. Anna set her down on her feet and picked up the water jar. They began walking back, keeping a steady pace until they reached the house. Anna stopped when she saw Oprah standing there, her gaze fixed on the stranger waiting at their door. Still several feet from him, Anna set the jar down beside Oprah, quietly instructed her to watch her sister, and approached cautiously. Going by his dress, he didn't appear to be Roman, but that was not always the case. Anna cleared her throat to get his attention. He turned towards her and smiled. Anna didn't recognize him but was calmed by his countenance: he had a kind face.

"I am looking for Anna, wife of Heli ben Matthat," he said simply.

"I am she."

He pulled a letter from his cloak and handed it to her.

"Elizabeth asked me to get it to you since I was passing through Nazareth."

Anna looked down at the letter. Even without opening it, she knew it was from Mary, asking to come home. This wasn't possible though. It was for her sake they sent her away, and if Mary was safe in Hebron, then she would stay there until the danger passed.

"*Shalom*," the stranger said, turning to leave.

Anna broke away from her thoughts.

"Forgive me; I am not being very hospitable. Can I get water for your animal? For you?"

He shook his head.

"I am just passing through."

"Thank you then…for bringing this."

"*Shalom*."

"*Shalom*," she reiterated as the stranger left, her gaze following after him. Oprah and Kyla approached her and took her hands.

25 *Sivan*

AS THE TIME FOR HER AUNT'S DELIVERY drew near, Mary helped the other family members with the preparation. Her uncle continued his studies, though he remained close to the house, for Elizabeth's sake. And just as Elizabeth's love was evident in her face, so was his love for her. Mary found herself contemplating that kind of love, allowing herself to think about Joseph, to imagine him as Zechariah, still in love with the wife of his youth after many years of marriage. And even though her mother had denied her request to return home, Mary hoped on the love she knew Joseph had for her, the love she had for him.

"Mary."

She looked up, aware she had been daydreaming again. The house was full of women, fussing over the very pregnant Elizabeth. Rona had taken charge of the chores and the meals, insisting Elizabeth rest.

"I've never seen anyone daydream so much," Rona declared.

"Leave her alone, Rona," Elizabeth said and paused, her discomfort obvious. She sat up and back into the chair. "She takes everything in, unlike you who talks too much."

The women laughed, as Mary smiled, happy to be a part of the group. Rona, though, narrowed her eyes and glared at Elizabeth.

"Oh, stop being so dramatic," Elizabeth continued and held her arm out. "Help me up."

Rona handed off the bowl of chickpeas to Mary and walked over to her cousin. She took Elizabeth's arm and helped her stand. Mary noted how big her belly looked, hanging lower now than it did even that morning.

"You should stay off your feet, *bat-doda*," Abigail offered from across the room, where she sat mending a gown. She was Rona's daughter, just a few years older than Mary.

Elizabeth paced to the door, her hand on her back.

"I feel better when I walk," she said.

"Well, you better get your rest now while you can, because you're going to need it, chasing a little one at your age," Jess stated. Mary recognized her from the synagogue, the wife of one of the Levites.

"I thought that's what you all were here for, to help me," Elizabeth laughed, resting against the wall.

"No, that's what you have young Mary here for," Rona said, sitting beside her again. Though they were family, Mary knew to not take Rona too seriously. The woman liked to talk, as Elizabeth said; no doubt one of the reasons Elizabeth stayed home for the first half of her pregnancy. Now that she was due to give birth; everyone was still talking, but it was about the miracle conception, just as they should be.

"No, Mary is here to learn," Elizabeth corrected her. "She'll be embracing her little one soon."

Abigail smiled and lay the gown on her lap. "If it's a boy, will you name him after his father?" she asked.

Mary felt her face get hot and picked at the chickpeas they would be preparing for dinner. This was something she had yet to get use to—being accepted as one of them. At home she was still a little girl and a helper, but here, she was a woman, with opinions and a mind of her own. They valued her words, even if they were few.

"We haven't talked about it," she said, truthfully. "Though my *achichem* was not named after my *abba*."

"When I have my first son, we will name him after his father," Abigail said, still smiling. "He'll look just like him and be just as sweet."

Some of the older women chuckled.

Jess ribbed the woman beside her. "Young love is precious, is it not?"

"What is wrong with that?" Abigail asked, offended.

"There is nothing wrong with love," Jess replied. "It's the husband you should ask about. Give Joachim a few years and see if you still feel the same way, after he has let himself go."

Another added, "And takes you for granted."

Still another said, "Or he doesn't talk to you or listen to you. See if you still love him after ten or twenty years of that."

Chatter filled the room as all the women started talking at once, comparing their husband's indiscretions and habits. Mary couldn't imagine Joseph doing any of those things, but worse was the expression on

Abigail's face: it was red and she appeared ready to cry. Mary looked around the room at her peers and decided to speak up. She cleared her throat and said, "*Doda* has been married for many years and she and *dod* are still in love."

The women got quiet. Mary felt her face grow warm again as all eyes rested on her. Then the women broke out in laughter. Mary didn't understand and tried to find reason in the faces around her.

Still laughing, Rona touched her arm and said, "Dear, your *dod* is…different; isn't that right, Elizabeth?"

Amidst the chatter, hers was the only voice missing. Rona turned to the door where Elizabeth stood, holding her belly, the expression on her face pained.

"Nothing to say?" Rona added, her voice light, though the concern was audible.

Elizabeth didn't respond.

All the attention was on her now, as she gripped the door and a puddle gathered at her feet.

"Elizabeth?"

Taking in a breath, she finally turned to everyone and stated, "The baby…"

Rona and Jesse rushed to help Elizabeth to her room as two of the other women ran for the midwife. Mary had been younger when Oprah and Kyla were born and only remembered the anxiety of not knowing what was happening…much like now. This was her opportunity to find out, well before she herself was to give birth.

As the chatter continued between the other women, Mary made her way to the room, staying out of everyone's way. She watched as Rona removed Elizabeth's dress, leaving her in her undergarment, a white, sleeveless gown that gave Mary a glimpse of her perfectly round belly and protruding navel. For a moment, Mary could only stare, until Elizabeth stiffened up and let out a muffled scream. She was shocked by her aunt's response; she was normally so calm.

"Mary," Rona called to her.

Mary tore her gaze from Elizabeth and turned to her. Rona motioned for her to come over.

"Walk with her," Rona instructed her.

And for the next hour, Mary did just that. While the midwife prepared for the birth, she kept step with Elizabeth, stopping when the pain struck, walking when it subsided. There were few words between them, and this was fine with Mary, as she was unsure of how to comfort Elizabeth.

"Bring her here," the midwife eventually stated, indicating the birthing stool.

Mary started towards her, her arm around her aunt's shoulder, but Elizabeth could barely walk. Her face was red with exhaustion and her body covered in sweat. Rona joined them, wrapping her arm around her back.

"Come on, cousin, you're almost done. You were there when all the others were born. It's your turn now," she said.

Elizabeth tightened her hold on both of them and nodded her head. They slowly walked over to the birthing stool and helped her sit down, pulling her undergarment above her belly. The midwife opened her legs, exposing her private area. Mary blushed and stood back as the midwife spoke softly to her aunt, encouraging her to push. Elizabeth did so, once, twice, three times, when the midwife exclaimed, "Your child is coming."

Mary watched as her aunt pushed once more, screaming with every breath. The head of the baby broke through the center of her womanhood. Elizabeth rested while the midwife cleaned the child's nose. She proceeded to hold down the head and instructed Elizabeth to push again. With one final thrust, the child was out and in the midwife's arms. She cleaned his face, causing him to wail, loudly.

"You have a son!" Rona announced, as Elizabeth relaxed against her.

Turning her attention to the child, Mary noted how the midwife wiped him down and rubbed a mixture of salt and olive oil on his skin. She cut the cord connecting him to his mother; then cleansed him with water and rubbed him down again, before wrapping him snuggly in a blanket and handing him over to his mother. Elizabeth's eyes lit up when he was placed in her arms, as though every pain she endured had been forgotten. She cradled him and stared down into his face, with a smile brighter than anything Mary had ever seen.

"Welcome, little one," she said, touching his face. "I've waited a long time for you."

3 *Tammuz*

STARING AT THE BLANK PARCHMENT before her, Mary considered what to write. Everything she had penned to her parents, up to this point, had been unsuccessful to her cause. What else could she say that would change their minds? What words could she use that would make them realize she belonged in Nazareth, not Hebron? That Joseph would not turn her away but embrace their new destiny?

Words failed her though and Mary set the pen down, feeling disheartened. She quickly chastised herself, though: Zechariah and Elizabeth's son was to be circumcised today. She had no right to walk around feeling sorry for herself. She had to pull herself together, so she could join them in the festivities.

Mary thought about the babe; he was perfect and perfectly formed. And his presence brought joy to everyone, especially Zechariah and Elizabeth. Zechariah remained deaf and dumb, despite the *malakh*'s words, yet this did not stop him from loving the child. The affection in his eyes for him was inimitable. He had begun spending more time away from his studies, enjoying the presence of his family for the first time in months; even smiling more, causing Elizabeth to beam. Mary had never seen her aunt happier than she was now and she knew it was because of what G-d had done for them.

A sense of peace enveloped her, and Mary rolled up the parchment. She tucked it away and stood. The letter could wait, she had a celebration to go to.

PRAISED ARE YOU, G-d our G-d, King of the Universe, who has sanctified us with your commandments and commanded us in the ritual of circumcision."

With Zechariah by her side and the family behind her, Elizabeth watched as the priest blessed her son, who was sleeping quietly in her brother-in-law, Shmuel's, arms. The emotions in her heart overwhelmed her: G-d had been good to them.

The priest moved to the table beside them and picked up a glass of *kiddush*. He blessed it and placed several drops into the baby's mouth to help him with the coming pain. Then he drank from the cup and passed it to Shmuel, who also partook of the *kiddush*. This was a symbol of their willingness to share in the child's pain. The priest then began the procedure, waking the boy in the process and causing him to cry. Every whimper broke Elizabeth's heart, but Zechariah comforted her by taking her hand in his and squeezing it tightly. She reminded herself that even though the pain was necessary, it was only temporary. Her son would be back in her arms shortly.

The priest completed the circumcision. Shmuel comforted the boy, and pronounced a blessing over him. This was a right usually reserved for the father, but because Zechariah still could not speak, Shmuel stood in his place.

"Blessed are you, G-d our G-d, King of the Universe, who has sanctified us with your commandments and commanded us to make him enter into the covenant of Abraham our father."

Together, everyone else replied, *"As he has entered into the covenant, so may he be introduced to the study of Torah, to the wedding canopy, and to good deeds."*

The priest continued his blessing.

"Creator of the universe, may it be your will to regard and accept this performance of circumcision, as if I had brought this baby before your glorious throne. And in your abundant mercy, through your holy angels, give a pure and holy heart to…" He paused for a moment, his gaze moving between Zechariah and Shmuel. "What is the child's name?" he asked.

Before Elizabeth could respond for her husband, Shmuel spoke up.

"Zechariah," he stated.

Elizabeth objected.

"No! His name is John." Though she had received the *malakh*'s words from Zechariah's penned description, their potency was still the same; and now having received the fruit of it, she was not going to disobey. John was the name G-d had given him before he was conceived, and it would continue to be his name now that he had entered the earth.

"There is no one by that name in the family, *achot*. His name should be Zechariah, after his father," Shmuel insisted.

"No," Elizabeth said firmly, shaking her head. "His name is John."

The mood in the room quickly shifted as the murmuring began. The same family members who were celebrating with them just moments before were now criticizing her lack of respect for Shmuel and for the process. The priest called for everyone's attention.

"What is the child's name?" he repeated.

Again, before Elizabeth could reply, Shmuel spoke up. He waved his hand at Zechariah and pointed to the child. "What would you name the boy?"

Zechariah looked at him blankly and for a moment Elizabeth feared he did not understand. Then he brought his hand up and made a swirling motion in the air—once, twice, three times before the others understood what he was trying to say.

"Get a tablet and a pen," someone instructed.

The talking increased, exasperating Elizabeth. This was not what she imagined for her son's circumcision. Mary turned to her, her expression sympathetic. She knew the truth and Elizabeth was grateful for her support, but it was the family, the friends and the neighbors who needed to know G-d had orchestrated these events—the conception, the birth and now the naming of the child.

John. The name meant 'G-d has been gracious' and that was the purpose to which he had been born, to show G-d's grace to his people. Yes, G-d had been silent for many generations now, leaving them to the whims of their *goyem* masters, but he was still there. He was still concerned for them. He had promises that had yet to be fulfilled, but would be, through her son and Mary's, the promised *Mashiac.*

A young child pushed through the crowd, carrying in his hand a tablet and a piece of coal. Zechariah received the items and concentrated on writing. Around him, the talking ceased as they waited to see what he would respond. Though Elizabeth knew he would back her up, a single thought crawled into her mind, causing her to worry.

What if he doesn't?

The *malakh* had said, *"You will become dumb and unable to speak until the day these things take place, because you did not believe my words, which will be fulfilled in their proper time."* The events had been fulfilled, yet he was still dumb. It seemed he had accepted his sin of doubt and offered penitence for it. Why then could he not speak? Why couldn't he hear? Why wasn't he healed of his affliction? Surely the birth signified the fulfillment of the *malakh's* words. Would G-d orchestrate all else and not return her husband's voice, especially now that it was needed?

ZECHARIAH STOPPED WRITING. Without any change of expression, he turned the tablet to the family and revealed his response:

His name is John.

Still holding the tablet, Zechariah mouthed the words that flow so easily from his soul:

His name is John.

That was what the *malakh* Gabriel had given him; had tried to tell him so many months ago and he dared to doubt the Almighty.

His name is John.

Now he was a father and the child, *his* child, was perfect.

His name is John.

He had doubted once, but never again.

"His name is John."

The voice speaking was hoarse, aged and unrecognizable. It filled the room and silenced everyone.

"His name is John."

Zechariah looked at the shocked faces around him. No one was speaking, but everyone was staring at him with amazement in their eyes. Even Elizabeth. He met her gaze, still mouthing the response requested of him. Her expression softened, and she smiled.

"His name is John."

In the silence of the room, Zechariah realized he was the one talking. It had been a year since he heard his voice, and, in his guilt, had forgotten what it sounded like. Still, that mattered none. Just as Gabriel had promised, he was a father and his son...his son...

Zechariah let the tablet fall from his hands and he raised his arms upward, praising the G-d who had not just heard, but answered his prayers.

"Thank you, *Adonai*," he stated, pouring out all the gratitude his heart held. Those in the room, from the old priest to the youngest child, held their tongues, listening with astonishment. "Praise be to you, L-rd, G-d of Israel. You have come to your people and redeemed them. You have raised up a horn of salvation for us in the house of his servant David, as you said through your holy prophets of long ago, salvation from our enemies and from the hand of all who hate us—to show mercy to our ancestors and to remember his holy covenant, the oath he swore to our father Abraham: to rescue us from the hand of our enemies, and to enable us to serve him without fear in holiness and righteousness before him all our days.

"And you, my child," Zechariah said, as he walked over to his son, John, who still rested in Shmuel's embrace. He reached for the boy and took him in his arms, holding him close to his bosom. The child whimpered, but was otherwise calm, tightly swaddled in his blanket. Zechariah was a fool to ever doubt G-d. This was a blessing only he could give.

He turned to Elizabeth, her face beaming with pride. He decided she was more beautiful now than the day he first laid eyes on her and moved over to her side. His gaze fell upon Mary, Elizabeth's young niece, and though he only had his wife's word on the matter, he knew the burden Mary carried…no, the blessing she had been chosen for—to be the mother of their savior! A great blessing indeed.

Zechariah turned his attention back to his son and continued, his voice cracking with emotion, "You, my son, will be called a prophet of the Most High, for you will go on before the L-rd to prepare the way for him, to give his people the knowledge of salvation through the forgiveness of their sins, because of the tender mercy of our G-d, by which the rising sun will come to us from heaven to shine on those living in darkness and in the shadow of death, guide our feet into the path of peace."

Elizabeth rested her hand on his shoulder. He looked into her eyes and saw the smile that had brought him peace these many years. John sighed loudly and settled in to sleep. And with that, the hush that had spread over the room was lifted. Everyone move forward, talking at once, wanting to know what manner of child this was, that G-d's hand should rest so strongly on him.

BACK AT HOME, Elizabeth paused for a moment, leaning against a chair to catch her breath. The household bustled around her, as she attempted to get ready for the midday meal. More neighbors and friends had joined them since word got out that Zechariah's voice had returned. Elizabeth knew they were there to gawk and gossip, but even that didn't distract from the joyous occasion: a son from barren loins and a husband restored to her. G-d was indeed good.

"*Doda?*"

Even in the noisy atmosphere, with Rona and Jesse boisterously throwing about commands, Elizabeth heard her niece's voice. She looked to her right where the girl was standing, her hands in front of her.

Mary's eyes were filled with awe—the same awe Elizabeth felt.

"*Dod* said we are ready to begin," Mary said.

"Good, good," Elizabeth replied, removing her apron. She set it aside and joined the others at the table. She sat beside Zechariah, who held their child in his arms. He met her gaze and smiled. Elizabeth returned the smile and waited for everyone to quiet down. With their attention on Zechariah, they listened as he thanked everyone for breaking bread with them but most importantly, for celebrating with them the miracles G-d had performed on their behalf. Elizabeth was sure they would speak of this day for years to come.

Zechariah raised his hand to silence the guests and turned his head upward to speak the traditional blessing following circumcision:

"G-d, help us to raise this child wisely. Give him strength and help him to grow up to trust in you and perceive you at the appointed times of the year. Thank you for the unhesitating hand of the priest who performed the circumcision to bring him into covenant with you. Send the Mashiac speedily and Prophet Elijah so that your covenant can be

fulfilled with the re-establishment of the throne of King David."

Cheers rose, and the talking began again. Some spoke of the miracle witnessed that day, while others talked of John—surely if his beginning was that wondrous, what would his life be like? Still others spoke of dumb Zechariah and barren Elizabeth as if they were still so. Elizabeth heard none of it, though. With one hand on John and the other on Zechariah, she quietly agreed with the blessing and said, "So be it."

17 *Tammuz*

ONCE AGAIN, MARY SAT AT THE TABLE in her room, staring at the blank parchment before her. She was done writing, though; done asking for permission. She was going home. However, this decision required disobedience and she had never rebelled against anyone, much less her parents.

What choice did she have, though? She enjoyed being with her aunt and uncle, but she needed to live her life, live the life G-d had called her to, and she couldn't do that in Hebron. Elizabeth's admonishments weren't lost on her and while she could admit being chosen of G-d was part of the reason behind her urgency to get home, it wasn't the only motive. Maybe she was being carnal, but she missed Joseph and she needed him to know about their new destiny.

Mary stood—she had to talk to Elizabeth and Zechariah. Leaving the parchment on the table, she made her way to her aunt and uncle's room, where she heard her uncle laugh. It seemed strange to hear his voice after months of silence

Mary knocked on the door.

"Come," Elizabeth said.

Mary entered and smiled at the scene before her: Elizabeth and Zechariah sat on the bed, with John between them. G-d could not have chosen more doting parents.

"He looks bigger today," Mary stated, walking over to them.

"As much as he eats, he ought to," her aunt replied.

"John is a healthy eater," Zechariah rebutted, even as his wife laughed.

"Listen to you. The boy is going to be spoiled," she said.

"No, he will be a good boy," Zechariah argued, an offended look on his countenance. "I will not dishonor *Adonai* by raising John any other way but according to his law, especially after everything he's done for us."

Elizabeth smiled and patted his arm.

"I know, my love. I know."

She kissed him.

Mary looked away, blushing.

"But you didn't come in here to see two old people kiss, did you, Mary?" Elizabeth said.

Mary turned back, a sheepish look on her face.

"No, *doda*."

Both eyed her expectantly. She took a deep breath.

"I think it's time…I mean, I'm ready to go home."

Elizabeth and Zechariah looked to each other. Mary couldn't read their faces, couldn't tell if it was disappointment, or worse, amusement. Mary felt her heart beat faster and her face get hot again. Surely they wouldn't deny her this…

Her aunt stood up, making sure not to disturb John, and walked over to her. She laid her hands on her shoulders and met her gaze.

"Are you sure?"

"Yes."

"Then we'll make arrangements."

Mary was glad for their approval, but there was still the matter of her disobedience.

"What about the fact that I am dishonoring my parents by disobeying them? They sent me here for a specific reason."

Zechariah rose slowly and joined his wife at her side. He took Mary's hand in his and gave her a reassuring smile.

"My dear, this is bigger than your parents; it's bigger than us. *Adonai* has set his salvation in motion and we cannot stand in his way. Though I am honored that he would allow you, the mother of our L-rd, to be here, you need to be where his plan is. There is no dishonor in that, no dishonor in following *Adonai*."

Mary was once again silent. Beyond their approval, she was glad for their love and appreciative of their understanding. It made her heart swell and all she could do to respond was hug them. Surrounded by their warm embrace, she knew she was doing what was best.

30 *Tammuz*

JOSEPH KICKED OPEN THE DOOR TO his workshop, his arms loaded down with wood pieces and tools. He had been called by the town miller to make repairs to his mill and would have been back earlier, but the miller liked to talk. Joseph had been gracious enough to listen, but talking wasn't in his repertoire as of lately, making the situation painful.

"How did it go?" his apprentice, Silas, asked.

Joseph turned around, dropping everything on the table.

"If I was paid for listening, I would never have to work again," he sighed.

Silas let out a chuckle.

Without another word, Joseph set about putting his tools away, relishing the silence around him. He grabbed his leather apron and tied it around his waist, before turning back around to Silas. He watched as the young man whittled away at the leg of a table he was building. He was younger than Joseph, but eager to learn the profession. Satisfied Silas was doing a good job, Joseph nodded to himself and returned to the chair he was working on before he was called away. They worked in rhythm and silence, until Silas suddenly interrupted.

"Oh, I forgot to mention: Rachel and her mother stopped by," he said.

Joseph groaned. Ever since Mary left, Rachel had been trying to get his attention. And now her mother was trying to match the two. He didn't normally run away from his problems, but this time, he saw no other solution.

"She was quite sweet, too," Silas added, with humor in his voice.

Joseph stopped working and rubbed his temples. He didn't need this.

"She's not coming back like last time, is she?" he asked.

"I don't believe so," Silas replied. "But you never know with a woman in love." There was a hint of mockery in his voice.

"Ugh," Joseph muttered to himself, then added, "I wish Mary would come back."

He picked up his knife, ready to focus on anything else but Rachel, when Silas said, "She is back."

Joseph stopped, unsure he heard Silas correctly. He gazed at the boy, who continued working, as if he had said nothing at all.

"What did you say?" Joseph asked.

Silas looked up at him. There was momentary confusion on his face before he replied, "I thought you knew. There was a caravan that came through earlier. She was with them."

It took Joseph a moment to fully comprehend that Mary, *his* Mary, was back. With his heart racing, he pulled his apron off and ran out of his shop. He turned back to let Silas know he would return later and rushed off to Mary's home. It had been months since she had left, and his heart ached for her. Joseph had not said the words before, but in her absence, he had come to understand he loved her. And now that she was back, he was going to tell her.

Joseph made his way to Mary's house, ignoring everything around him. He quickened his pace, anxious to see his betrothed. The walk seemed to drag on, until he finally turned the corner and saw her house. Mary was standing out front with her family, the youngest two jumping up and down in excitement. He stopped and smiled, his heart beating wildly now. Taking a deep breath to calm himself, Joseph started toward them, considering what he could say that would not betray his excitement. But the closer he got, the more he realized this was not a happy reunion he was witnessing: Anna was frowning as Heli talked in hushed tones.

Then Kyla threw her arms around Mary.

"I want to see your baby," she cried out loudly. "Show me your baby," Kyla repeated, running her hand over Mary's midsection.

Joseph stopped, confused.

Everyone noted his presence now.

"Joseph!" Heli said, his voice abrupt.

But Joseph didn't hear him. He was focused on Mary…and her baby?

JOSEPH HAD BEEN inside Mary's house only once before, when he spoke with Heli about marrying his daughter. But even then, he was not attentive to the modesty of it. Just a basic home, one story, with three rooms: a bedroom for the children, one for Heli and Anna and a main room for cooking and communing. It was a spacious room, not unlike his; it just struck him as odd that he was noticing all this now, as Mary was explaining her 'situation'. Really, he didn't know what else to call it, with all her talk of *malakhs* and the *Mashiac*. He was a good Jewish man, who believed in the G-d of Abraham, Isaac and Jacob; and went to synagogue and prayed daily. But to believe his betrothed had been impregnated supernaturally? Joseph's eyes wandered around the room, trying with all his might to distract himself from Mary's voice. Just an hour earlier, it was all he wanted to hear. Now, he couldn't even stand the sound of it. She had betrayed him and expected him to believe this nonsense—an incredible feat, considering not even her parents believed her. He could see it in their expressions, their body language: Heli stood propped against the back wall, his hand covering his mouth, while Anna anxiously wrung hers, and paced back and forth, looking everywhere but him. If they didn't believe Mary, why should he?

Joseph rose to his feet, startling Mary and silencing her. They made purposeful eye contact. Her big, black eyes stared back at him, seemingly pleading for understanding and acceptance, but he could offer neither, not anymore. He had gone there to tell Mary he loved her, to tell her how much he looked forward to her return, how much he desired to take her as his wife, to build his life with her; but with Mary's admission of her pregnancy, her betrayal, her sin, the life he had imagined was gone. His heart weighed heavy with that realization, and though he had never been emotional, he found himself fighting back tears. It was time to go.

"Joseph?" Mary whispered, reaching for him.

But he turned away from her and, without a word, walked out of the house.

ANNA CLOSED THE door to the children's room, her mind still consumed with the day's events. She lit a candle to banish some of the darkness and set it on the table. Then she followed the well-trodden path she had laid into the floor with all her pacing.

The door opened, startling her. She stopped and held her breath, fearful of whom it might be, but it was only Heli. She was relieved, until she met his eyes. There was an uncertainty in them that she was not familiar with and it scared her.

"Did you talk to him?" Anna asked.

Heli shook his head, before turning to shut the door.

"Joseph wouldn't speak with me."

He walked over to the table and dropped into a chair. Anna followed him.

"How's Mary?" Heli asked, his tone softer.

"Asleep, finally. The child would not stop crying. She expected Joseph to accept everything she said." Anna spoke with disbelief in her voice, the thought ridiculous to her. "I just don't understand why she came back. She should have stayed with Elizabeth; she would have been safe."

"It doesn't matter anymore," Heli stated, with a sigh of resignation.

"No, it does matter. There must be something we can do."

"It's out of our hands, Anna. Joseph will decide Mary's fate now."

2 *Av*

˝ARE YOU GOING TO EAT?˝

Joseph snapped out of his thoughts and looked at the bowl in front of him. Barley soup, his favorite; yet tonight, he had no stomach for it.

"I'm not very hungry," he admitted.

"How can you not be hungry? You worked all day at the shop," Miriam exclaimed. She stood over him, making him feel like a boy again, even though he was the man of the house. "It's that girl, isn't it? I told you courting her was a mistake. She—"

"No, *Imma*," he interrupted, mostly out of habit, though he wasn't ready to confess his lack of appetite was about 'that girl'. "It was a long day, that's all. I appreciate the meal, but I think I will just turn in."

He rose, hoping she would let the subject drop, but she didn't.

"I worry about you," Miriam said, the edge gone from her voice. "You work too hard. And with Mary leaving and returning and the rumors I hear—is she really a wise choice for a wife?"

He had argued this point with her many times before, always defending Mary. And it wasn't that Miriam had anything against Mary specifically—in her opinion, no one was good enough for Joseph. He was sure she would have accepted Mary by the time of the *nissuin,* but now with everything that happened, it seemed her concerns had been valid all along. Mary was pregnant and Joseph wasn't the father. He was under no obligation to defend her anymore, much less marry her.

"Joseph?"

He leaned down and kissed his mother on the cheek.

"You don't have to worry about that anymore. There won't be a wedding," he said and left Miriam at the table. She called him back, demanding clarification, but he simply went up the stairs to his room and closed the door, so he could not hear her. With a long, hard sigh, he lay down on his bed and stared up at the ceiling.

There would be no wedding, Joseph finally understood that. But he'd be lying to himself if he said it was because Mary had betrayed him. For days now, Joseph had been racking his brain, trying to come up with reasons Mary would seek the comforts of another man. Joseph wasn't perfect, but he had done what he could to show her that he wanted to be her husband. And Mary seemed to want him as well, she seemed to be content to be his wife. Had he missed something then? Joseph was sure he hadn't. More than that though, he was certain he knew Mary, knew the type of woman she was. His attraction to her aside, he knew she was a good and loving person; she was kind and honest. She was introspective: she didn't say a lot, but took things in, understood what others needed and how she should conduct herself. She was filled with *binah* even now. And if that was the case, then this could only mean that Mary was telling the truth: that she had been chosen by G-d, impregnated by his holy spirit and was now carrying his seed.

If Joseph was any kind of man at all, then he could admit that this was the reason he couldn't wed Mary. After all, she was G-d's handmaiden. She accepted his word and his destiny for her life. She would birth their long-awaited savior, nurture him and raise him the way Jewish mothers had done since time immemorial. Where did that leave him then? What was he supposed to do? If he did proceed with the wedding, what could he offer G-d? How could he possibly be any kind of father to the son of the Supreme one? How was he supposed to raise him? What could he teach the *Mashiac* that he didn't already know?

Joseph felt like he had been given a glass to view himself, only to find his reflection lacking. He wasn't worthy. He was nothing but man, formed from dust, short on faith and grace. He couldn't measure up to Mary's level of belief, and he certainly couldn't bring her down to his doubt.

No, there would be no wedding. But that still left Mary: what was he to do about her? Bring her before the priest to end the marriage contract? Admit that she was pregnant? That would be a death sentence for her. She would be stoned according to the law. Joseph couldn't do that. Even if he couldn't marry her, he still loved her. He would just have to annul the engagement and let her go away quietly somewhere to have her son.

The words pained him, even as he thought them, but it could be no other way. He had to take himself out of the picture and learn to live with that.

Joseph wanted to be glad for the decision, instead of waffling back and forth between his thoughts, but he felt worse. Hoping to find some relief, he rolled over towards the wall and waited for sleep to take him, even as he ignored the nagging voice that called his name in the darkness of the room.

MARY AWOKE AT the first sound of thunder. Not in the far distance, but right outside, it seemed. She jerked up into a sitting position, unsure of where she was for a moment. Then she remembered she was home. The thought was not as welcoming as it should have been. She heard the pitter-patter of the rain outside and lay back down. It was only a storm.

She closed her eyes to try to sleep again but was interrupted once more by a pounding outside. Someone was knocking on the door.

The knocking continued for a few more seconds before it was followed by a voice.

"Mary!"

She didn't stir, afraid of what would follow. She heard her mother anxiously whispering, as the pounding continued.

"Mary!" the voice cried again, and for a moment she thought she recognized it. "Mary, please, I need to talk to you."

Yes, she knew who it was—Joseph.

She got out of bed, as someone lit a lamp in the other room and opened the door. Mary looked briefly at her brother and sisters, who continued to sleep soundly, and wondered how they could do so in all this noise.

Perhaps it's best this way, she told herself. The last couple of days had been stressful for everyone. On the urging of her mother, they had stayed inside, avoiding the neighbors and busybodies who would no doubt contribute to the rumors floating around about her if given the chance. Nathan understood, but the girls were constantly asking why, something Mary had begun asking herself.

The house was quiet again. Mary tip-toed towards the door and without a sound, she opened it enough to see her father talking to Joseph. He was dripping wet and his expression was more emotional than she had last seen on him. All talking ceased as they realized Mary was up. They glared at her, seemingly in confusion; and for a moment, she didn't know what to make of the situation. Then her father stepped back, giving Joseph permission to approach her.

Mary opened the door to her room and stepped out, closing it behind her so as not to disturb the other children. Joseph walked up to her, leaving a trail of water behind him. He stopped in front of her and took her hands. She couldn't tell if it was tears or rain that wet his face.

"Mary, I am so sorry..." There was shame in Joseph's eyes, in his tone. "I've spent the last two days trying to come to grips with...I mean I didn't know how to take your news. I wanted to believe that...I thought you had betrayed me, but tonight, as I prepared to sleep, or as I slept, I'm not sure which it was, I..." He seemed reticent to continue, dropping his gaze to her hands. He paused for a few moments before continuing. "I opened my eyes and there was a man, a very tall man with hair like the sun and skin like jewels. This man was standing in my room. As I beheld him, I knew I was in the presence of one who sits at the feet of *Adonai*. Then he greeted me: 'Joseph, Son of David.' Before I could say anything, he said, 'Don't be afraid to take Mary as your wife because what has been conceived in her is by the Holy Spirit. She will give birth to a son and you are to name him Jesus, because he will save his people from their sins.' Then he was gone."

Joseph paused again, as if struggling to find the right words. "Forgive me. I thought to divorce you quietly, to send you away, but that is not where my heart is. I want us to be wed. Mary, I want you to be my wife."

Mary was struck by how surreal the moment was. Two days before he had rejected her. Now he was begging for her forgiveness. More than that, he wanted her, child and all, destiny and all. Her heart swelled and she squeezed Joseph's hands.

"Of course," she replied, and for the first time since her arrival, Joseph smiled.

MARY SAT ON her parents' bed, listening as Joseph and her father talked. The hour was late, yet plans had to be made—plans for her future.

Anna walked into the room, leaving the door ajar and joined her on the bed. Mary leaned into her, resting her head on her shoulder, as her mother put her arm around her. Neither spoke, glad for the reprieve they'd been given.

"Mary, I'm sorry," Anna eventually said. "I'm sorry I didn't believe you."

Mary nodded. As good as it felt to be vindicated, this was not something she needed to hear from her mother in order to forgive her. She knew everything Anna did was based on love and while it would have been nice for her mother to believe her when she first told her, what counted was that she believed her now.

Unexpectedly, Anna sat up and stared at Mary.

"I'm going to become a *savta*, aren't I?" she asked, with sudden realization.

Mary responded with a chuckle.

"I guess I will need to write to Elizabeth too. I've missed so much because I wouldn't believe. You said she had a boy…?"

"His name is John."

"That's a good name," Anna said, then fell silent again as she drew Mary to her.

It occurred to Mary that this would be the last time they would sit there as just Mother and Daughter. She would be a wife before the day ended, joining Joseph at his home. And in a few short months she herself would become a mother.

She sighed with contentment and closed her eyes.

3 *Av*

JOSEPH WALKED BACK TO HIS HOME. It was nearly dawn and though he should have been tired, he wasn't. He had much to do to prepare for his *nissuin*. It would not be the grand thing he had once thought it would be, but the end result would be the same—he was bringing Mary home as his wife.

The thought had his heart ready to burst. Mary, his wife. After the visitation from the *malakh*, he could only think about making the situation right, driving him to leave his house in the middle of the night in a rainstorm to apologize to her. G-d had confirmed everything, and let him know that what Mary said was true, but he also gave him a sense of peace that he had a role to play in all this. He didn't know what it was, but he understood he needed to obey. More than that, it was also a gift—regardless of what he felt, he could continue to love Mary as a husband.

"You. Stop."

Joseph instinctively obeyed, all thoughts of elation gone. He didn't have to turn around to know it was a Roman soldier. In his excitement to see Mary, he had forgotten about the dangers of going out late. There was no curfew but because of the unrest in the population, many Jews were stopped and questioned after sunset. Most were merely sent on their way; some, though, were killed, their bodies left on the side of the road for the birds.

Not wanting to provoke the man, Joseph remained still and waited for him to approach, praying it wasn't trouble he wanted.

"Who are you?" the man asked, as he circled round Joseph, intimidatingly.

"Joseph ben Jacob. I'm a carpenter."

"And what is a carpenter doing out this early?

"I...I went to see my betrothed."

The soldier looked him up and down, his eyebrow arched. The man was broad across the shoulders, adding to his menacing appearance.

"I thought you Jews frowned upon such behavior," he asked, mockingly.

However true his comment, Joseph realized too late what his response sounded like. He wanted to retract his statement; this was the last thing he needed to say, for Mary's sake. If the priests and elders heard about this...

A second soldier came running up to them, his metal gear clanging with every step. He greeted the first soldier, then turned to Joseph.

"You're the carpenter, right?"

"Yes."

"You do good work. You made that chest for me." Speaking to the first soldier, he added, "You've seen it, the one with the carvings."

Joseph recalled the face now. He glanced at the first soldier, hopeful the recognition would earn him a pass, and indeed it did, as the second soldier admonished him, "Go on your way, Carpenter; but next time, conduct your business during the daylight."

With a nod of agreement, Joseph hurried back to his house, his steps fast upon the dirt. He heard laughter from the soldiers, most likely at his expense, but he cared not—this was another day he got to live.

THE DAY BROKE, turning the dark sky purple, then blue. Inside her home, Miriam blew out the candle as light began streaming in through the window. Tired of pacing, she took a seat at the table and watched the door, willing Joseph to come home. His strange behavior at dinner was cause enough for concern, but when he left abruptly in the middle of the night…well, all she could do was worry.

She shook her head. How long had she been sitting like this? How long had she paced the floor? From the time he was a boy to now, all she did was worry for him. Was he eating enough food? Was he working too hard? Did he choose the right girl to marry? A mother's work was never done.

The door suddenly opened and before Miriam could even stop herself, she rose from her chair and exclaimed, "Joseph," not knowing if it was him or not. When she saw it was, she rushed to him and hugged his neck. He was taller than her short, rotund body and smelled of perspiration, but that didn't stop her from pulling him down to her level to hold him. She was glad he was alive and safe.

"Where have you been?" she demanded, releasing him so she could see his face.

Joseph offered her a tired glance before letting his arms drop to his side.

"I went to see Mary," Joseph stated quietly.

Miriam's mind stopped racing with worry and entertained anger instead.

"Why? You said last night there would be no wedding!"

"I know, but—"

"Your father and I didn't bring you into the world to go sneaking around like this. It was her idea, wasn't it? She's beguiled you somehow—"

"Stop—"

"I knew she was no good for you, all those rumors floating around about her and strange men—"

"*Imma*, enough!"

The severity in his tone made her stop. He pointed to the chair and pled with his eyes for her to sit and listen. Miriam complied. Joseph knelt in front of her.

"Mary hasn't beguiled me. I know last night I said there would be no wedding, but that was before I understood fully what the situation was."

With a deep breath, Joseph told her about Mary being pregnant with the *Mashiac* and about his 'visitation' the night prior. His words were sincere, but Miriam could clearly see how lost the boy truly was. He had been duped by this girl and now she was going to saddle him with her bastard child.

"This is why you should have listened to me in the beginning," she stated, sadly. "Making up such stories of *malakhs* and now she fancies herself worthy of being the mother of the *Mashiac*? You are not going to marry her. We'll talk to the priest and—"

Defiance settled across Joseph's face and he firmly countered, "No."

"But it's obvious she's lying!"

He shook his head and rose to his feet.

"My mind is made up. I love Mary and I want her to be my wife. Besides, this is the will of *Adonai*."

At that, Miriam laughed bitterly. Will of G-d, he said. Did he even understand what that meant? It was nothing but a tired cliché, something people threw around when they didn't know what else to say.

"We'll see how much of this is *Adonai*'s will when the people find out what she's done."

The defiance on his face was replaced with fear and anger and Joseph knelt in front of her again.

"You can't say anything about this to anyone," he instructed.

She started to laugh again; however, his expression warned against it.

"Promise me!" he demanded.

Now Miriam was the angry one, but Joseph was so settled on the matter, she knew she would not win this argument with him. He was determined to marry the girl. Though she knew in her heart he was making a terrible decision, she nodded her head in agreement, biting her lip to keep from saying anything contrary. She would let him have this, but that didn't mean Mary would escape her wrath.

STANDING BESIDE JOSEPH in his house, under the *chuppah*, Mary's stomach flutter-ed, much like it did early in her pregnancy. There was no nausea this time, though; only nervousness, happiness, contentment and excitement rolled into one. Not even Joseph's mother's hard expression was enough to change her countenance.

Mary looked around as the *rabbi* read from the *ketubah*. She noted how different this ceremony was from the first one, her *erusin*. Then, they were joined by family and neighbors to celebrate the engagement. Now, it was only her family, Joseph's mother, and Silas and his family, who served as the necessary witnesses. The event seemed meager but viewing the pride on her parent's faces was enough to lift Mary's heart and remind her that this was more than tradition. She and Joseph had been chosen by G-d for a grander purpose and didn't need the fanfare that normally came with it.

With cup of *kiddush* in hand, the *rabbi* began reciting the *Sheva Berakhot:*

"Praised are you, O L-rd our G-d, King of the Universe, creator of the fruit of the vine.

"Praised are you, O L-rd our G-d, King of the Universe, who created all things for your glory.

"Praised are you, O L-rd our G-d, King of the Universe, creator of man.

"Praised are you, O L-rd our G-d, King of the Universe, who created man and woman in your image, fashioning woman from man as his mate, that together they might perpetuate life. Praised are you, O L-rd, creator of man.

"May Zion rejoice as her children are restored to her in joy. Praised are you, O L-rd, who causes Zion to rejoice at her children's return.

"Grant perfect joy to these loving companions, as you did to the first man and woman in the Garden of Eden. Praised are you, O L-rd, who grants the joy of bride and groom.

"Praised are you, O L-rd our G-d, King of the Universe, who created joy and gladness, bride and

groom, mirth, song, delight and rejoicing, love and harmony, peace and companionship. O L-rd our G-d, may there ever be heard in the cities of Judah and in the streets of Jerusalem voices of joy and gladness, voices of bride and groom, the jubilant voices of those joined in marriage under the bridal canopy, the voices of young people feasting and singing. Praised are you, O L-rd, who causes the groom to rejoice with his bride."

Still holding the cup aloft, the *rabbi* bade Joseph to drink. Mary watched as he took the cup and obeyed. When he was done, he passed the cup to her and she drank as well, finishing the wine before returning it to the *rabbi*. With a broad smile across his face, he took the cup back and declared them one flesh, amidst the cheering of her family and Silas'.

MARY KEPT HER head down as Joseph led her to his room—their room now, he reminded himself. Her modesty was charming; she could barely look him in the eye. She was, no doubt, anticipating, like him, what was to come next, the consummation of their marriage.

Yet even as he shut the door, leaving their family and celebration downstairs, Joseph found he was not as excited as he should have been, and not because he didn't want to be with Mary. There was something different about her, something special. She was still the same girl, yes, but knowing she was chosen of G-d to carry the *Mashiac* …well, who was he to venerate her as anything less? To treat the mother of the *Mashiac* as ordinary and pretend he knew what it would be like to be a husband to someone like her? The fears he entertained the night before came rushing back and Joseph started to doubt his place in this marriage. But he knew he couldn't do that. The *malakh* had told him this was the will of Adonai, and even if he wasn't sure there was anything he could offer, he had to proceed forward. Mary needed him, perhaps only for protection, but she needed him.

Still facing the door, Joseph took a deep breath and turned around. Mary stood quietly in the middle of the room, her hands in front of her, her gaze down. She shifted her weight from one foot to the next.

"Mary," he said quietly.

She eyed him uneasily, before looking back down. He cleared his throat and began again.

"I know we've been betrothed for some months now, but since everything has

occurred so quickly, I thought…I mean, perhaps we…*you* would feel more comfortable if
we waited until you were more…com-
fortable. I mean with this being so sudden…"

She gazed up at him again, no longer
with worry or concern.

"Really?"

Joseph nodded, relieved with her
acquiescence.

"Until you're ready," he reiterated and
stepped closer to her. He took her small,
smooth hands into his calloused ones.

"I like this," Mary admitted, with a shy
smile, "when you hold me. I'm ready for
that."

Joseph smiled and pulled her in closer.

4 Av

MARY OPENED HER EYES AND STRETCHED out her arms. The room was quiet, and she was alone. Joseph had gone to morning prayer, leaving her to sleep in. She shook her head, feeling guilty, but not for very long. A smile crept up on her face at the thought of Joseph. She couldn't have asked for a better, more patient husband, who was willing to wait until she was ready. She would adjust soon enough, but until then she didn't have to worry or feel anxious about anything.

After dressing and saying a quick prayer, Mary made her way downstairs to the main room. The house was bigger than hers—*my parents'*, she corrected herself—and while it would add to her chores, it wasn't anything she couldn't handle.

"Did you sleep well?"

Mary turned around towards Miriam, who was standing at the worktable gazing at her. Her voice was grave and humorless; and her demeanor, anything but friendly. Then Miriam's eyes dropped to her midsection. Mary shifted her own gaze downward, uncomfortable with the scrutiny.

"I…I did," Mary stammered.

"I didn't wake you when I went to get water or start the cooking, did I?" Miriam asked with a measure of sarcasm in her voice, "Because the chores will not do themselves when the woman of the house sleeps in."

Miriam glanced at her once more before turning back to the table and going back to rolling out the dough for the day's meals.

Mary was too hurt, too embarrassed to respond.

18 *Av*

THE DAY WAS ALMOST OVER, MARY noted to herself, as she prepared the evening meal. She wiped the sweat from her brow and plated the roasted meat. Setting it carefully on the table, she stopped to make sure everything was perfect—for Joseph, but for Miriam as well. The woman was difficult; nothing seemed to please her. The situation wasn't so bad when Joseph was home, but now that he had returned to work after the completion of their marriage week, she was left to fend for herself. Mary would rise early, clean the house on her own, go to the well and prepare the food—all in hopes of getting Miriam's acceptance. Nothing helped though. Miriam always had a sarcastic or biting comment ready. She even accused her of trapping Joseph in marriage. Mary tried to argue; it was all useless though, the woman never listened.

Mary sighed. The whole situation was frustrating, but she had to deal with it.

Miriam was her mother-in-law and deserving of honor. Mary would be bringing shame on her if she went to Joseph and complained. She was supposed to be his helpmeet, not a burden, especially when she considered everything he did for her. It wasn't until Mary returned from Hebron that she saw what G-d's call meant for Joseph and the sacrifices he had to make on her behalf. She could not take that lightly.

A sudden uneasiness in her midsection distracted her from her thoughts. She rested her hand on her belly and took in a deep breath until the discomfort subsided. She was starting to show. Soon enough she would look like her *doda* did, giving her mother-in-law another reason to despise her. Mary was flustered by the thought, but quickly forgot about it when Joseph walked in. She smiled and rushed to his side. He returned her smile and put his arm around her.

"Such a warm welcome," he stated.

Mary blushed.

"I'm glad you're home," she admitted, shyly, truthfully.

"I'm glad to be home," he responded quietly. Their eyes met; and for a moment, there was something 'unspoken' between them.

Then Miriam walked in from her room.

"Joseph," she said and moved between him and Mary. Joseph greeted her and kissed her cheek, leaving Mary standing off to the side. Miriam walked him over to the basin, so he could wash his hands before they sat down to eat. Mary was upset to be set aside so easily, but she reminded herself that, at the very least, Miriam's focus was off of her. This was enough to be grateful for; and with Joseph present, the woman wouldn't openly attack her.

GOING BACK TO work was harder than Joseph imagined. When he wasn't with Mary, he spent his days thinking of her. He understood now why King Solomon wrote, *a man who found a wife found a good thing.* She served him gladly, cleaning and cooking for him during the day and spending time with him in the evening—and all without complaint. Being with child was not easy and he knew his mother could be hard to get along with. Still Mary seemed to handle it all skillfully. She was a gift to him, and he appreciated that, especially now as she removed his sandals to wash his feet. It had been a long day, most of which was spent working on his feet. Although Joseph had objected to Mary performing the task, she insisted on it. He couldn't deny he felt better now, though.

Mary stood upright, offering him that shy smile he had come to associate with her. She gazed at him as she did earlier when he came home and again, he was entranced by her...

With suddenness, Mary placed her hand on her belly and let out a small cry.

"What's wrong?" Joseph asked, reaching for her.

Her face went from shock to surprise. Then the corners of her mouth inched up, forming a smile.

"I felt the baby," she said with awe in her voice. Before Joseph could say anything, she took his outstretched hand and placed it on her belly, the most intimate they had been. He felt the warmth of her body beneath his hand; and for a moment, he forgot why he was touching her.

Then he felt it, a jab against his hand. It was just slight enough to be noticeable and Joseph looked away from Mary's eyes to her belly. Something was in there. No, some*one* was in her. The *Mashiac.*

"Did you feel it?" she asked in the same tone.

Joseph looked up at her again. He wanted to say yes, to take her in his arms and hold her but feeling the child only made Mary seem more intangible. She was chosen of G-d. She carried his seed. She had no need of Joseph.

He nodded his head, releasing his hold on her.

18 *Heshvan*

"GIRLS!" ANNA CALLED AFTER HER daughters.

They stopped briefly, waiting for her to catch up. But their attention was soon captured by an insect hopping into the path. They followed after it, forgetting their mother behind them. Anna sighed and gave up trying to keep pace with them. With the jug on her hip, she proceeded towards the well, her strides slow and steady. She was lost in her thoughts, thinking about the day ahead of her.

Before she arrived at the well, she heard voices, women talking and laughing. Anna groaned, not caring to partake of anyone's company today. She usually tried to arrive early enough to avoid her neighbors, but with two little girls in tow, it was extremely difficult to do so.

Anna pushed forward and saw three women in the distance, one of them Mary. She smiled. Always glad for a chance to see her daughter, she quickened her pace. Oprah and Kyla found another insect in the distance to entertain them and didn't see their sister at the well.

The closer Anna got, though, the more she realized not all was well. The other women, Rachel and another girl from town, whom she didn't recognize, were harassing Mary. Anna's instincts kicked in and she rushed forward. Rachel was the first to notice her and offered a charming smile. Mary seemed relieved to see her mother.

"*Shalom*, Anna," Rachel said.

Anna skipped the niceties and stated, "Go home, girls," as she placed the jar beside the opening of the well.

"We have as much right to be here as you do," Rachel insisted.

"Where are your jars then? Or are you just here to bother an innocent girl?"

"She's hardly innocent. Look at her. Look how big she is. Whose child is she carrying? Is it Joseph's? I think she tricked him into marrying her."

Anna turned to her daughter. Her opinion biased, she couldn't help but smile to see how beautiful Mary was. Her face had filled out with the expansion of her belly and her countenance was glowing. Anna returned her attention to Rachel and replied, "Envy does not look good on you, Rachel. Now go home and stop bothering Mary."

Rachel's mouth fell open, but no words came out. Obviously offended, she turned around and left in a huff, her friend following after her.

"You know they won't stop," Mary uttered, the sorrow in her voice unmistakable.

Anna knew the truth of the matter, yet she wanted to believe that the others in town would stop talking about Mary and Joseph, that they would stop troubling Mary when she was out and that life for her oldest child would return to normal. She didn't know how that would be possible, given what G-d had called her to; however, this was her prayer. At the very least, Anna could cheer Mary up. She straightened up and put a smile on her face.

"Never mind them. How is my *nekhed?*"

Mary placed her hand on her belly and replied with a smile, "He's very active. All he does is kick, sometimes day and night."

The thought of Mary as a mother was still foreign to Anna, but accepting G-d's role in this affair, following Joseph's visitation with the *malakh*, made it all more…palatable. In truth, she couldn't help but marvel, not just at G-d, but also at the transformation of her own faith. And she was more than happy to be a doting *savta*. Placing her hand on top of Mary's, Anna said, "Well now, he's going to have to slow down some to give his *imma* a rest, isn't he? How is Joseph?"

"Well."

"And Miriam?"

Mary didn't respond.

Anna sighed.

"I'm sorry I didn't believe you. Perhaps your situation wouldn't be as bad if I had believed and you had talked to Joseph sooner—"

"It's not your fault, *imma*. You couldn't have changed any of this."

Anna knew she was right. Still, when she thought about it, she couldn't help but feel it was her disbelief that made things worse for Mary. What if, what if, what if…ultimately, though, it did them no good for her to think that way. She had to be practical.

"Have you talked to Joseph about his mother?" Anna asked.

Mary shook her head.

"He works so hard without complaint, even though people talk about him and this child, because of me. I don't want to bother him."

Anna gave her a soft smile.

"Mary, you are still young, so I want you to listen and tuck this away in your heart. You are blessed and highly favored, regardless of what others have to say. *Adonai* has chosen you, but he has also chosen Joseph. I think you know that, otherwise, you wouldn't have fought so hard to come back. That means you aren't alone in this. You don't have to bear this burden by yourself. Let him be there for you, in the good and bad. We have no guarantee that any of this will get better, but *Adonai* has given you his grace to make it through all of it. He's given you his grace to survive."

Though she had been intent in her listening, Mary now smiled.

"*Doda* would often speak of *Adonai*'s grace. She said it didn't assure success, but meant he was working through our lives."

Anna mused, "My sister always had greater *binah*."

Mary nodded in agreement.

"Mary, talk to Joseph. He loves you and will see to it that you are well-cared for," Anna advised.

Mary seemed hesitant, but she finally said, "I will."

21 *Heshvan*

WITH EVERY STEP THEY TOOK, HELI wondered why he didn't drop Nathan off at home after leaving the synagogue. The boy had a habit of talking a lot when it was just them, which puzzled him greatly since he was usually quiet at home. Whatever the reason, Nathan took no notice as Heli veered off the path they usually took and headed towards the western side of the market, where Joseph's shop was located. Anna had shared her concerns about Mary and Joseph and asked him to speak to Joseph. Though he saw him often enough at the synagogue, he thought it would be best to speak to him at his shop instead, knowing they would not be able to find any privacy otherwise. People liked to talk, and though it pained him to hear what was being said of his daughter and son-in-law, he knew there was nothing he could do to sway public opinion.

"Well?"

Heli looked down at his son, who stared up at him with expectancy on his face, a face that reminded him of Anna, with her deep, dark eyes and soft features. Not knowing the question Nathan had posed of him, Heli simply said, "Uh huh."

"Don't say 'Uh huh.' I know you weren't listening. Where are we going, by the way? Home is back the other way and I'm hungry. Do you think *Imma* will make her sweet bread this morning? Hopefully Kyla will leave me some. She always eats most of it and Oprah…"

Heli smiled, even as he groaned. Nathan didn't notice though and continued talking as they wandered through the marketplace already bustling with life. They arrived at the carpentry shop, a small building, modest in appearance, adjacent to the stables and the farrier.

"Do you think Joseph will let me carve something?" the boy asked.

"I don't know," Heli said, though it would be a good distraction for the boy. He opened the door and ushered his son inside before following him in. Joseph and Silas were already at work.

"*Shalom*," Joseph greeted them.

"*Shalom*," Heli returned.

Nathan approached Joseph's worktable, his eyes filled with wonder and fascination. Sitting on the table were several wooden toys: a cart, a horse and a little boy, all exact replicas of their larger models.

"You made those?" he asked, gently handling the cart.

"Silas and I did," Joseph replied proudly.

Nathan said nothing else, taking turns admiring each piece. Heli chuckled to see the boy finally speechless.

"So, are you just visiting, or can I help you with something, Heli?" Joseph inquired after a moment.

"Just visiting. I wanted to check up on my favorite son-in-law," Heli replied, tongue-in-cheek. He turned to Silas and asked, "Perhaps you can take Nathan next door to the farrier to see the horses?"

Silas concurred, even as Joseph's demeanor changed, something akin to curiosity and tension. Once they were gone, Heli turned to Joseph and pointedly asked, "So how are you and Mary doing?"

Returning his attention to the carvings in front of him, Joseph said, "We're good."

Heli watched him, recognizing the response for what it was—a brave front.

"I've heard the talk, Joseph, so I know you and Mary are aware of it. You don't have to pretend for me. This has to be difficult for you both."

Joseph locked eyes with him but seemed reticent to respond. Finally, he said, "Can I ask you something?"

"Of course."

"How did you know you would be a good father to your children?"

Heli considered the question for a moment.

"Honestly, you don't know until the child is born and you behold them for the first time. Whatever you felt earlier, whatever questions you had before, in that moment you know you will do anything in the world for them."

Joseph hesitated again.

"You're a good man," Heli said, trying to encourage him.

"Perhaps but how do you father the *Mashiac*? How do you teach him? *What* do you teach him? I am only a carpenter."

"It's a good profession. It was your father's profession."

"I know, and that's fine because I was only supposed to be a carpenter. I wasn't meant to be the savior of our people. So how can I teach him that? How am I supposed to be any kind of father to him?"

"The same way you will when it's your flesh and blood."

At that, Joseph stopped working. He continued to hold eye contact with Heli, but the older man could tell there was something else, something more eating away at his soul.

"Heli, I love your daughter, but...when I look at her, I don't see a wife or mother, only what is out of my reach. She is patient and loving and well-equipped for this call, while I...am not. To be honest, I fear touching her or beholding her in anyway but revered."

Heli's heart broke for his son-in-law. He had known him since he was a boy, when he was apprenticed to his father in this very shop. In the months since Mary returned from Hebron, Joseph had endeared himself further to the family. For his generous heart and even-keeled demeanor, but admittedly for protecting Mary. Surely, Joseph had to know what a blessing he was...but as the young man continued to gaze at him, searching for assurance, Heli realized he didn't understand his value.

"Son, it's not just Mary who is favored; you were just as chosen as she was. Understand that a husband and wife are no longer two people in the eyes of *Adonai*, but one. He didn't choose Mary and then choose you. He chose you both. He blessed you both. He favored you both. And truthfully, she needs you as much as you need her. I'll tell you, I could not survive without my Anna. I was incomplete until I met her. She is my other half; my better half and I know you feel the same for Mary. What *Adonai* has asked of her, he asked of you. You are both in this together. We are all in this together— you, Mary, Anna, me and Miriam."

Joseph said nothing. There was still doubt in his face, but now there was a sliver of hope accompanying it.

"Talk to Mary," Heli admonished him. "You may find she's more human than you behold her to be."

After a long moment, Joseph finally said, "I will."

23 *Heshvan*

STRUGGLING TO FIND A COMFORTABLE spot, Mary rolled over to her other side. The position was slightly better, but not by much and certainly not with the child moving around within her. It seemed lately he had his days and nights mixed up. This provided for relative peace during the day, but when the evening came, she had trouble eating, had to constantly relieve herself and now, she couldn't get sufficient rest—all because he was constantly moving around. Still, even as she thought about it, she marveled at the changes her body had gone through to accommodate the child; and soon, real soon, she would be holding the fruit of those changes. She would be a mother and Joseph, a father.

In the moonlight, Mary could see Joseph's body outlined on the floor. He had chosen to sleep there since the night of their *nissuin*. Even with some bedding and several blankets, she knew it had to be uncomfortable, but Joseph respected her wishes to wait. Mary was humbled by that. Some-times she wondered why G-d had chosen her. It was obvious why he had selected Joseph. He was thoughtful, caring and patient. This made talking to him even harder. She had tried to do so that first night after her mother admonished her to share her concerns with him, but the words never came. Then Miriam spent the next evening 'attentive' to her son. And with Mary turning in early almost every night, it was close to impossible getting Joseph by himself.

But Mary knew those were just excuses. She had G-d's grace; there were times she didn't think she would survive the harshness of this season, yet she was still here. And G-d had surrounded her with people who cared for her: her parents, her *dod* and *doda,* and now Joseph. Despite her situation, she had to talk to him.

Mary let out a soft sigh.

Soon...she would talk to him soon.

JOSEPH HEARD MARY sigh and envied her. Not exactly the right response as her husband, but she seemed to be able to rest in spite of the harshness of the season...something Joseph couldn't do. Despite volunteering to sleep on the floor and insisting he was fine with it, Joseph's back was telling him this was a bad idea. Mary was his wife after all. He should be sleeping with her.

But he couldn't.

But I should, he thought to himself. Grateful to have a father-in-law as wise and as caring as Heli, he reflected on the conversation they had only a few days earlier. Joseph knew the words were truth, but he couldn't get past his feelings.

Mary needs you.

Only to protect her from being stoned to death.

No, she wants you as much as you want her.

But she's with child by G-d.

She's the same Mary she was before.

But she's carrying the Mashiac and you're to be the savior's father.

Joseph sighed and rolled over on his other side. His back hurt less this way…for now. He knew he needed to talk to Mary, it was the only way he was going to get any peace; but with his mother consuming his time at home and Mary turning in early due to the strains of her pregnancy…

I'll talk to her soon, he promised himself. *Soon.*

25 *Kislev*

THE SUN HAD BROKEN OVER THE horizon, spreading its warmth to everything in its path, including Mary, who was already sweating from lugging the water jar from the well. She didn't want to stop as she was almost home; however, she couldn't take another step. She set the water jar down and rested. Mary placed her hand on her belly and tried to quell the uneasiness inside her. She thought she had gotten big when she was six months along, but now that she was in her ninth month, she couldn't believe how much more she had stretched out. How big was this child to get? The day of her fulfillment was soon; still if he delayed any longer, she wouldn't be able to do anything. As it was, Mary found herself waddling, not walking. And carrying anything, much less a full water jar was difficult...though she did use her belly as a make-shift shelf some-times.

The thought made her chuckle and Mary decided it was time to head home, before her absence provoked Miriam. Mary had yet to talk to Joseph, but…

The clanging of metal caught her off-guard. The sound was subtle at first, then it increased, sounding almost like a thunder-ous herd steadily moving towards her. Mary quickly picked up her jar and moved away from the road leading into town. Then *it* appeared over the horizon—first one head, then another, then a detail of Roman soldiers, all marching in formation, their metal swords clanging against the rest of their gear. She watched in shock as they began parading past her. She had seen soldiers before; indeed there was a company stationed there in Nazareth, but never this many: rows and rows of men, with their stoic faces, marching forward into her town, her country.

A hand rested on her shoulder, causing Mary to jump. She looked back, expecting to see one of the foreigners, but it was Joseph. He placed his arms around her and pulled her closer to him, protectively. Around her, other townsfolk started congre-gating to watch this procession—women, children, men; they were all there and all bore the same anxious expressions.

What's happening now? She wondered, as her gaze returned to the soldiers, still marching past them.

28 *Kislev*

THERE WAS FEAR IN EVERYONE'S EYES lately and Joseph was no exception. The Roman presence in the area had increased exponentially and with the escalation came a decree requiring all men to register in their hometowns.

"They're going to tax us to death!" a man shouted.

The men from Nazareth had filled the synagogue to talk about this latest development. Many were angry, and all were scared, though few would admit it.

"This is nothing but a tactic from the *goy*. They want to know how many of us there are, so they know how to destroy us," another yelled.

"What do we do about it?"

"We fight!"

The last response achieved its intended effect, and the men began shouting. This was dangerous, though, considering the soldiers who were now stationed in their town.

"*Achichem!*" The voice was barely audible in all the noise, but it was persistent. "*Achichem!*"

The noise began dying down.

"*Achichem,*" the voice cried out again. It was the town miller. "This is not the time for fighting. We must wait on the *Mashiac*; the conditions are ripe for him to come."

This elicited another round of angry responses. Some cried that they couldn't wait that long, while others said there was no *Mashiac;* that they had to fight and free themselves. Joseph said nothing, figuring this was not the time or place for it. Would they want to hear that the savior was in their midst? More than that, would they be content to know he was not what they wanted, but a yet-to-be-born babe? What purpose could he serve with soldiers lining the streets of their town?

"Listen!" another voice boomed from the front. Joseph recognized it as Heli. "Listen. Regardless of what you feel right now, the miller is right: this is not the time to fight."

A young man approached Heli, his fist in front of him, his stance defiant.

"And when is? When we have our beloved *Mashiac* to lead us? We've been waiting on him for centuries and still he doesn't come. Instead we are enslaved by one *goyem* after another. *Adonai* has turned a deaf ear to our suffering. We cannot wait."

Not moved by the man's speech, Heli replied, "We are few; they are many. We are laymen, millers, smiths and carpenters; they are soldiers. We are emotional, they are organized. They would cut us down in an instant, and where would that leave our wives and children and even grand-children?"

Silence permeated the room. Joseph watched his father-in-law proudly.

"*Adonai* is not deaf, nor is he sleeping. Like the psalmist said, *Your Protector will not slumber. Indeed, the Protector of Israel does not slumber or sleep.* Is this a test, then? I don't know. What I do know is that *Adonai* still works, and he still cares, in spite of our disbelief. The time is always ripe for a savior, but we must look for him in the right place. And right now, that place is not the end of a sword."

With that, the arguing was done, which for Joseph meant the course had been set: he would be traveling to Bethlehem to register.

THE MOOD WAS somber as Mary waited for Joseph. The men had been called to a meeting earlier that afternoon and now with the sun setting and no word from them, Mary couldn't help but worry. What if the *goyem* walked in upon the meeting? What if they decided the men were conspirators against Caesar? No proof was needed, just the word of a Roman citizen. And it wasn't as if their king, Herod, would provide back-up or demand restitution if something happened. Everyone knew he lined his pockets from the coffers of Rome.

Frustrated, Mary got up from her chair and walked over to the window. With the meal cooked and the table set, she had nothing left to distract her.

"You used leeks again to season the goat? You know I don't like them," Miriam sharply stated as she inspected the meal. Mary knew Miriam was speaking out of worry; still it didn't stop the words from stinging.

"Miriam, I—"

She didn't have a chance to apologize as the door opened suddenly. It was Joseph and he didn't look happy.

"What happened?" she asked, rushing over to him. He put his arm around her and pulled her to his side.

Miriam asked, "What did they say?"

"All the men are to register in their hometowns, according to their clans and tribes," he replied.

Mary could hear the defeat in his voice.

"That's ridiculous," Miriam stated.

Joseph released Mary and walked over to the table. He took a seat and sat back, letting his shoulders slump.

"They honestly expect you to go to Bethlehem?" his mother continued, as she paced the floor around him. "Lose almost two weeks' worth of wages just to accommodate them?"

Mary perked up. He would have to travel to Bethlehem?

"Why do you have to go there?" she asked.

Miriam glanced at her with scorn, as if she should know better than to interrupt.

"That's where my father and his house hail from," Joseph responded.

The City of David. Now she understood why the *malakh* had addressed him as the Son of David so many months ago.

"The shop will have to close. Silas will have to register as well," Joseph pondered. "I can make the trip in less time, but that will mean traveling by myself."

"Oh, no," Miriam objected vehemently. "You will do no such thing. Even if it extends your trip, find a caravan to travel with; there is safety in numbers. You can stay with your cousins there, your father's people, and then find another caravan to get home."

Mary's heart started palpitating wildly. She would have to spend two weeks or more with Miriam? No.

"Joseph...can...I go with you?" she asked.

Miriam answered for him.

"No! There is no reason for you to go. Your place is here."

Sarcasm underlined her comment. Mary hoped Joseph would argue, or at the very least, notice it, but he didn't.

"*Imma*'s right, Mary. With the day of your fulfillment close, it's best for you to stay here."

Mary knew she had to obey her husband, but there was no way she was going to last two weeks alone with Miriam. She had to talk to Joseph.

WEARY FROM THE day's activities, Joseph made his way up the stairs to his bedroom. Each step was a heavy one and he was ready for sleep. Mary had gone up an hour earlier and it was just as well: the last few days had been stressful.

But when he walked into the room, he found she was still up.

"I thought you'd be asleep," he said, shutting the door.

She rose from the bed, avoiding eye contact, her hands searching for something to hold.

"Joseph…I…"

He saw the angst in her face and approached her, beginning to feel anxious himself.

"What is it? Is it time for the child?"

She shook her head.

"No. No. I just…can I talk to you?"

Joseph relaxed.

"Of course you can."

Not knowing what to expect, he sat down with her on the bed. Mary was quiet at first, her eyes firmly on her hands in front of her. Then the words begin to flow. She wanted to go with him to Bethlehem. He was ready to argue against it until she told him about his mother's attitude and behavior towards her. He began to get upset, angry with his mother.

"How long has this been going on?" he asked her sharply.

"Since the *nissuin*," she said, still avoiding eye contact.

"Why didn't you say something sooner?"

She shrugged and finally looked at him. There was fear in her eyes, the level of which he hadn't seen since the day she came back from Hebron.

"I thought I shouldn't complain. She's your mother and you've been so good to me. I mean, I've made it this far with *Adonai*'s grace. I didn't want to trouble you, especially since you work hard for me and for this child and he's not even yours. You've been rightly chosen for this task and while I can never doubt that this was *Adonai*'s doing, I am beginning to see that this was not all the glory I thought it would be."

A tear streamed down her face and for the first time in the last few months, she seemed a little more fragile, a little more…human.

"I always thought you were the one rightly chosen," he told her, softening his tone. "You have great patience and *binah*. I doubted, while you believed."

Mary laughed.

"I don't think I had a choice but to believe," she said, pointing to her belly.

He chuckled and asked, "Can I tell you something?"

She nodded.

"I've been afraid," he began and shared his fears and hesitations with her. The expressions on her face ranged from disbelief to incredulous, but still she listened, offering him solace, instead of pity. His heart swelled and Joseph appreciated her even more.

"I don't deserve any kind of veneration," she said.

No, not veneration, Joseph thought, but definitely love. He took her hand, daring a look into her eyes. She returned his gaze, and they were lost for a moment. Without any more hesitation, he leaned forward, his lips drawing closer to hers. He wanted to kiss her, as his wife, the way he should have after their *nissuin*, but not before he told her, "I love you, Mary."

Her response was quick and sure.

"I love you, Joseph."

His lips found hers and they kissed for the first time. It was everything he imagined it would be.

"Joseph," Mary stated, when the kiss ended.

He gazed at her.

"I probably won't be ready until the child is born, but...would you share the bed with me now?"

"Yes," he replied, leaning into her again, then added, "And yes, you can come with me to Bethlehem."

3 *Tevet*

"NO, SHE CAN'T GO WITH YOU TO Bethlehem!" Anna stated, visibly upset.

Joseph had left the shop in Silas' care to talk to her about his trip. He had expected her to react, but not like this. Still, he was determined to stay strong in his decision. Mary was his wife, and until he had a chance to make sure his mother was treating Mary as a daughter should be treated, he was not leaving her there while he made the trek to Bethlehem.

"She's due any day now," Anna continued.

They were in the main room of her house, where Nathan, Oprah and Kyla were eating, watching him with the innocent curiosity that children possessed. It had been unnerving at first, when he began courting Mary, but slowly they had warmed up to each other.

"I understand your concern, but Mary is strong," he replied. "She can make the trip just fine. Plus, I want her with me. I think it's best that way."

"For you or for her?" Anna retorted.

Joseph sighed. He was loathed to admit it, but he had to.

"For her."

Anna's demeanor changed; her face was not as hard, and her shoulders relaxed. She seemed to understand what he was trying not to say, and rather than respond to him, she turned to her son and said, "Nathan, take your sisters outside."

Kyla whined.

"But I'm still eating."

"Your food will still be here," Anna assured her, helping her out of her chair. "Go with your brother just for a few minutes."

Kyla obeyed, but pouted the whole way out.

"And how is Miriam taking this?" Anna asked, turning her attention back to Joseph.

"Not well. I had hoped in the beginning she would accept Mary and the child, but…"

Anna rested her hand on his shoulder.

"She needs time, that's all."

He sighed.

"I hope so."

"Trust me, once she meets the little one, she'll forget everything else."

Still focused on his own misgivings, Joseph didn't agree, yet he didn't argue either, knowing Anna was saying this for his benefit.

"So, what can we do to help?" she asked.

"I don't want *Imma* to be by herself while I'm gone. I thought perhaps she could stay with you. I would compensate you, of course."

"That would be unnecessary. You're family, you and Miriam. Of course she can stay."

"She will not be pleasant," he warned her.

"I can handle her," Anna said. "Just keep my daughter safe."

Joseph noted the expression on her face, the softness of it in the mention of her daughter. She reminded him of Mary and in a small way, Joseph was comforted, knowing everything would work out for the best. G-d's grace, Mary had said. G-d's grace indeed.

5 *Tevet*

TO MARY, IT SEEMED AS IF ALL OF Nazareth was traveling somewhere to register. Many of the faces in the caravan were familiar ones; while at home, the streets were a lot emptier than they normally were. Or at least they had been that morning, when she and Joseph left.

The tension was strong as Mary set up camp for the night. She listened to the chatter of the men nearby. They talked about the Romans, the registration and the coming revolution—nothing she hadn't heard before. Still she wondered if this was it, the time when her people would rise up. The *Mashiac* was in their midst; surely that was a sign of things to come, right? That one day he would lead them in overthrowing their Roman masters?

Deciding it best not to think about such things, Mary prepared dinner: dried meat and day-old bread. It wasn't the ideal supper, but it would keep them until their arrival in Bethlehem in three-days' time.

Joseph returned from gathering wood as she managed to lower herself onto the ground. Mary made herself as comfortable as possible on the bedding, knowing she likely wasn't getting up—not without help, at least. Resting her hands on her belly, she watched as Joseph tended to the fire.

With the work done, Joseph sat beside her and put his arm around her shoulder. They ate in silence, listening to the others in their group carry on. Mary considered for a moment how she and Joseph would be replaying this scene for the next few days.

That's fine, she decided, laying her head on Joseph's shoulder. As long as they were together.

10 *Tevet*

THE DONKEY KICKED UP GRAVEL FROM the road, causing Mary to cough.

"Are you alright?" Joseph asked, stopping the animal.

She cleared her throat and nodded her head, not wanting to worry him. He had been considerate of her from the time they left Nazareth and never complained, even when they fell behind schedule and lost step with the caravan because of her.

"I'm fine," she managed.

"We can stop and rest if you need to," he offered.

She shook her head.

"No, I can continue. I would like to walk, though."

Mary held out her hand and Joseph helped her down. She joined her husband in leading the animal towards Bethlehem. They were not too far now; still it seemed they had been on the road for weeks, their pace painfully slow.

She put her hand on her back. It had been hurting for the past couple of hours and she hoped by walking, she could alleviate it. A sudden pain hit her abdomen and Mary stopped, reaching her arm out to Joseph. She took a hold of him and squeezed.

"Mary?"

After a long moment, the pain subsided, and she released Joseph's arm. She had been experiencing pressure in that area for two days now, but this was the worst it had gotten…almost like the pain her *doda* felt when her time of fulfillment came, and John was born.

Her breath caught in her throat as the realization hit her—the child was coming!

No, no, no, she thought, her hands on the underside of her belly, as if to hold him in. *Not now!*

"Mary, what's wrong?"

The concern in his voice was unmistakable, as was the apprehension in his eyes. Mary didn't have to tell him she was in labor—he saw it and with a nervous push towards the donkey, he said, "Come on, we're almost there."

HIS CONCERN NOW panic, Joseph rushed to his cousin's house in Bethlehem. It was dark and late; and Mary's pain had intensified to the point where she couldn't walk. He had to leave her next to the well, holding onto their donkey as he ran to the door. He could see her outline in the light of a bright star overhead, but it wasn't enough to quell the anxiety growing in him.

His heart beating loudly, Joseph knocked on his cousin's door and waited. Joseph was a boy the last time they saw each other; and he wasn't sure the man would recognize him, or even remember him. He just prayed he would be able to accommodate him and Mary. It seemed everyone in Judaea had arrived in Bethlehem to register. Even now, he could hear voices and laughter of people gathered inside of the home.

Joseph pounded on the door when no one immediately responded.

The door swung open and a burly man appeared.

"What?" he asked with disgust.

"Cousin Eli," Joseph breathed out with recognition.

The man raised an eyebrow and eyed him suspiciously.

"It's Joseph, Jacob's son," Joseph explained quickly.

Eli looked him up and down, as if trying to remember him.

"Jacob's boy, huh?"

"Yes."

The suspicion left him, but he didn't move or welcome Joseph in.

"You here to register?" he asked him.

"Yes," Joseph replied.

"Unfortunately, we have no room," the older man said. "The rest of the family arrived last night."

Joseph's heart fell.

"Is there no space at all?

"See for yourself," Eli stated and moved to the side to allow Joseph to peer in. The main room was crowded with people, young and old. The older family members were seated, while the children played on the floor. There was an air of familiarity, but also annoyance. This was not a happy reunion.

"Perhaps if we had known you were coming..." Eli continued, letting his words trail off.

Joseph shook his head.

"There was no time to send word. Then we fell behind the caravan..."

"We?"

Joseph started to respond, when a heavy-set woman approached them from inside and asked, "What's going on? Who is it?"

He didn't recognize her, but going by her boldness, he figured her to be Eli's wife.

"This is Jacob's son, my cousin," Eli said to the woman. "He's here to register, but there is no room left."

"Please," Joseph pleaded, "If it was just me, I wouldn't care. But my wife is in labor."

He stepped back to give them a view of Mary, who was holding the underside of her belly, a pained expression on her face.

The woman's countenance softened.

"Oh dear," she said, and turned to Eli. "We can't send them away."

"Where are we going to put them?"

"There are a couple of stalls in the barn. They can stay there for now until something opens up."

Eli turned to him, and shrugged his shoulder, as if to ask him if he wanted to do that. Joseph sighed. The barn wasn't the most ideal lodging, *but* at least they would be inside.

"Alright."

WITH HIS ARM around Mary's waist, Joseph walked her slowly into the stables.

The smell of manure was strong; and for a moment, Joseph reconsidered his decision. Then Mary stopped. Her eyes were tightly shut, and she ceased breathing as her body tightened up. Joseph was afraid for her; yes, he had told Anna she was strong, and he still believed that, but this all seemed more than even he could take.

"Well, come on, you don't want the baby to birth itself, do you?" Eli's wife said, coming up behind them. Carrying some blankets, a candle and a stool, she walked past them into a clean stall and started setting up for the birth.

When Mary's pain decreased, Joseph resumed walking and led her over to where the woman was. Feeling helpless, he could only watch as she helped remove Mary's veil and untied her belt.

"Out with you, now," the woman said, still helping Mary undress.

"Should I...?" Joseph began, but he couldn't think of a single thing he could do to help.

"I've birthed six children. Your wife is in capable hands," she assured him, then sternly added. "Now go."

Without an argument left, Joseph walked back outside, unsure of what to do. He could be a patient man when required; however, he wasn't sure he could handle waiting. Seeing Mary in pain was the worst experience of his life, though he couldn't imagine it was any better for her. If that's what childbirth was about, he was grateful he wasn't a woman.

Joseph decided to take care of his donkey while he waited. He found his way back to the well, where the animal rested. He relocated him to the stable entrance and tied him to a post, awaiting permission to take him inside. He unloaded their bags and brushed him down. With the task done, Joseph sat down beside the entrance. A dog wandered over and sat beside him. Appreciative of the company, Joseph stroked his coat, pondering what to do next. His stomach was tied in knots, so eating was not an option. He thought about going inside to talk to Eli or the other family members, but it didn't seem right to socialize while Mary was going through labor.

A scream emerged from the barn. Joseph jumped to his feet, ready to rush in but he hesitated after giving it some thought. Was something wrong? Or was this all part of the process? Eli's wife would have come to get him if something had happened to Mary, right?

There was another scream. Joseph stepped into the barn, then back out. He wanted to go to her and help her, rescue her, take the pain from her, but he knew he couldn't do any of that. This was part of the natural course of things, what it took for a child to be born into the world, and he simply had to wait. Joseph sat back down beside the dog and pet him. As if wanting to comfort him, the creature moved closer and rested his head on Joseph's lap.

Time and time again over the next few hours, Joseph had to quell his instinct to protect Mary. She had become his other half, as Heli said, and to hear her suffering was more than he could bear. Joseph began to pray; however, the words were barely out of his mouth when he heard another cry, a different one: it was the cry of a babe, a newborn. Struck by the sound of it, Joseph stood up and made his way to the stall where he left Mary. There he found his wife, sitting on the stool. She was dressed in her undergarments only; her legs were uncovered and there was blood on the nearby straw; yet she was wearing the biggest smile he had ever seen. She gazed up at him and that's when he noticed the bundle in her arms.

Her son, he thought, then corrected himself: *their son*…the *Mashiac*. Apprehension gripped his heart once again.

Mary moved the blanket away from the child's face as Joseph stepped closer to her. Reminding himself of his father-in-law's words, he took in a deep breath and knelt beside Mary. She leaned into him, so he could take a closer look at the boy. He was small, pink and wrinkled, with a head full of black hair.

"Isn't he beautiful?" Mary whispered.

Having been struck speechless, all Joseph could do was nod. Foolishly, he had imagined the child would be born with the full wisdom of a man and the knowledge of his destiny. And maybe somewhere in his consciousness, the babe was aware of it. For now, though, he was simply a child, perfect in shape and form, just as G-d created him. He would fulfill his calling in time; until then, Joseph would accomplish his and be the boy's father.

"What will you call him?" the woman asked.

"Jesus," he replied, gently stroking the child's head.

11 *Tevet*

THE HOUR WAS LATE, BUT MARY remained awake, watching Jesus sleep in his make-shift bed. The woman who had assisted her had bundled up several blankets and placed them in the manger, giving him a place to sleep off the hay and away from the animals.

"You should sleep too," Joseph suggested, standing behind her.

"I like watching him," she replied, taking his hand in hers. "He's so full of peace."

Joseph knelt beside her.

"You've had a long day, what with the birth and the pain and labor…"

Mary chuckled.

"You know, I've forgotten what it all felt like."

He gazed at her, his eyebrows arched in disbelief. Mary blushed and smiled innocently. She wouldn't have thought it possible, but when she held her baby for the first time, the struggle she went through to have him was lost to the blessing of holding a new life. Mary squeezed Joseph's hand and leaned her head on his shoulder. Everything felt right.

Then a voice interrupted their peace.

"Is that him?"

Mary and Joseph looked up. Behind them stood three men and a boy. Two of them were carrying shepherd's crooks, but there were no animals with them.

"Is that him?" the older one of the visitors asked again.

"Who?" Joseph released Mary's hand and rose to his feet.

"The *Mashiac*," he replied. "We were told we would find him here in the stables, sleeping in a manger."

Shocked, both Mary and Joseph looked at the boy, who continued to slumber soundly.

"Who told you this?" Joseph asked, turning back to the shepherd.

The man seemed hesitant to respond, but with a nod from his companions, he said, "We were out in the fields near here, keeping watch over our flock, when a *malakh* appeared before us. We were terrified, but he greeted us and said, 'Don't be afraid. I've come to bring you great news. Today a savior was born for you in the city of David. And this is a sign for you: you will find a baby wrapped in swaddling clothes and lying in a manger.' Then, as he finished speaking, there was a multitude of *malakhs* behind him, filling up the fields and the heavens, singing, 'Glory to G-d in the highest heaven and peace on earth!' And as suddenly as they appeared, they disappeared. We said to each other, 'We need to go to Bethlehem and see this thing the L-rd has made known to us.'"

The shepherd ended his tale with an expectant look on his face: was this him, their savior?

Joseph glanced back at Mary and then stepped aside to give them access to their *Mashiac.* Mary sat up, protectively, then forced herself to relax. After all, Jesus did not belong to just her and Joseph: he was born for all.

THE LIGHT BEGAN to break through the darkness when the shepherds finally left. They had beheld the child and praised G-d. Mary said little throughout their visit, wondering if this was how their lives were going to be. Was this part of the grace G-d had bestowed on them, part of the honor she and Joseph should expect because they were the parents of the *Mashiac*? Just as Elizabeth had told her months before, there was no precedence, no standard for their lives. So, what should she expect? Would they have any semblance of normalcy or would it always be one visitor after another, coming to venerate the child? Eventually he would grow up; what then? Did he know now he was born to save his people? Or would he grow into that knowledge?

Only time would tell. Right now, Mary was content to tuck the questions away into her heart.

"You should sleep now," Joseph admonished her again. He had walked the shepherds out and was now kneeling beside her and the sleeping Jesus.

"What about you? It's been a long day for you too and you still need to register," she replied.

"There'll be time for that. You just get some sleep until we can get a room. I'll keep watch over you both."

Mary nodded her head.

"I love you," he said, softly.

"I love you," she whispered back and kissed him on the lips before lying down beside the babe and shutting her eyes.

About the Author

Ruth E. Griffin began telling stories at a young age, first with pictures, then with words. Though she considers herself an artist first, she wrote her first book as a teenager and has continued writing since then. Ruth is now the award-winning author of several fictional and non-fictional books, which center on women's experiences. She is also the founder of Studio Griffin, a full-service vanity press. A New Jersey native, Ruth now resides in North Carolina with her husband. They are parents to four adult children. Her books are available at all major online bookstores. Visit www.ruthegriffin.com for more information. Email her at ruthegriffin@outlook.com.

9 781736 176528